Quickies – 9
A Black Lace erotic short-story collection

D1638696

Look out for our themed Wicked Words and Black Lace short-story collections:

Already Published: *Sex in the Office, Sex on Holiday, Sex in Uniform, Sex in the Kitchen, Sex on the Move, Sex and Music, Sex and Shopping, Sex in Public, Sex with Strangers*

Published August 07: *Love on the Dark Side: A Collection of Paranormal Erotica from Black Lace* (short-stories and fantasies)

Quickies – 9

A Black Lace erotic short-story collection

BLACK

LACE

Black Lace books contain sexual fantasies.
In real life, always practise safe sex.

This edition published in 2007 by
Black Lace
Thames Wharf Studios
Rainville Road
London W6 9HA

The Art of Fucking	© Nikki Magennis
Public Relations	© Mathilde Madden
Pickup Girl	© A. D. R. Forte
Union Blues	© Monica Belle
Cabin Pressure	© Maya Hess
Wet Walls	© Kristina Lloyd

Typeset by SetSystems Limited, Saffron Walden, Essex

Printed and bound in Great Britain by CPI Bookmarque,
Croydon, CR0 4TD

ISBN 978 0 352 34155 6

The Art of Fucking
Nikki Magennis

My flatmate couldn't even imagine the desert that was my sex life. She leant back in her chair, swinging her long tanned legs. Sandy's body always seemed to fall beautifully into place – wherever she was, the room would arrange itself round her. She looked like Botticelli's Venus, only with more lipstick.

If Sandy was a classic Italian painting, I was an abstract expressionist mess. As we sat in the sun-filled kitchen, sharing tea and our Sunday hang-overs, I compared the two of us.

Not a good idea. My short fingernails were rimmed with dark-blue paint, a perpetual stain which never seemed to scrub off my hands. Sandy's were shining and polished, and just long enough to suggest they'd been raking over a man's back all night long.

They had. The night before, Sandy had scored.

'An absolute raging beast,' she said. 'He fucked like a tornado. I mean howling and screaming all the way.'

In fact, I'd heard the howls of the raging beast and the rattling of Sandy's headboard in the small hours. I'd covered my head with a pillow and tried to block it out. Just another loud reminder of how different Sandy's life was from mine.

I'd lain awake for a few hours, wondering how the hell I'd ended up where I was.

I'd just moved in with Sandy after splitting up with my live-in boyfriend, and was still adjusting to life in a shared flat. Sandy's wild lifestyle and messy habits intimidated me, so I spent most of my time in my studio. It was a dingy building in the wrong end of town; a quiet, cold ten feet square space where I wrestled with my own obsession – painting.

It was a difficult beast, and fickle too. I needed a truckload of expensive and potentially lethal poisonous materials, plenty of uninterrupted solitude and the right kind of light.

North light. You need a flat even light that doesn't splash itself over the canvas or turn orange at the end of the day. A steady source that is never brash and never surprising. It felt like my life was lived in a constant north light. The smells of turpentine, linseed oil and white spirit surrounded me. After a day in the studio I'd be giddy with fumes, the colours of the street outside on the way home would shock me. Nothing I painted could ever compete with the noise and the huge blast of electric reality that confronted me when I stepped out into King Street. I painted big canvases, used strong colours, threw daring shapes into the compositions. It never quite clicked. My life was all about reflecting what I saw, trying to show the huge terror and beauty of the world. But I always felt like I was watching from the sidelines, painting half-hearted pictures of a life not fully lived.

Sandy, by contrast, lived in the eye of a beautiful storm. I'd been amazed at how fast she tore through men. She bedded whichever passing guy caught her fancy, discarded them afterwards like used tissues, moved on to the next one. And I? I was still stuck in the melancholy aftermath of heartbreak, still attached to my ex, unsure of how to change or of exactly what I needed. Knowing I needed something.

'A good fuck', was Sandy's opinion. Inevitably, for a woman who relished every juicy, sticky detail of a one-night stand, her answer to all life's problems was a good fuck. Now, I was a little naïve when it came to loveless encounters. I guess I was a romantic at heart – I liked the slow build-up, the shy smiles and late-night conversations. I liked to feel it was meaningful before I fell into bed with someone. Steady, gradual. Sex like the north light, no surprises and no brief flashes. The smell of love in the air before I joined my body with a man's. I didn't know if I could sleep with someone I didn't love, though it made me feel old-fashioned to say it.

'But who says it's not love?' Sandy threw her hands in the air like she was tossing my morals aside. 'There's a hundred kinds of love out there, honey, a different one for every person you meet. Why not try tasting a little sample of what's possible? A mouthful of fun? An adventure, even. God knows, you could use a little excitement.'

Monday I trooped to the studio as usual, to face the current work in progress. I uncovered the palette. Limited to three colours at the moment – raw umber, Prussian blue, a little squeeze of scarlet. I was working on an interior, a picture of a kitchen. Just a table and chairs, a window, the angles of the walls. Simple, quiet, shadowy. The kind of room you could sit in and be alone with your thoughts. I was working up the background, layering washes of thin paint over each other until the colours merged into a muddy neutral depth. Deepening the shadows. I plugged in my Walkman – I like to listen to something dark while I'm working. Mazzy Star played some haunting guitar chords, and I dipped my brush into the turps. Softened the bristles, rubbed at the squeeze of blue paint till it melted into a liquid pool. Approached the easel and faced the canvas, hand poised over it, ready to make a mark. I saw where the colour needed deepening, and started work.

And then I was joined, hand moving with eye, locked into a space where no one could touch me. Wordless, nothing but the light and the colour and the resinous smells of the studio, music washing straight into me, suffusing me with steel guitar and a voice singing songs I knew so well I didn't even listen to the words. Painting an imagined room, losing myself in a place that didn't exist.

* * *

The hand fell on my shoulder like a thunderclap. I jumped so high I knocked the edge of the turps tin with my hand and saw the splash of dirty blue water explode over the floor, the palette, my jeans. I looked up to meet the startled gaze of the guy who'd just touched me. In my ears, some old electro song was still playing, and I felt like I was still locked in the dream state with a stranger intruding rudely into my headspace. He had the grace to look upset – a pale face with blue eyes that were cracked with shock and concern. Delicate lips that were moving fast, forming words I couldn't hear.

'What?' I said, pulling the earphone away. The cold sound of real life rushed against my ear, mixed with the sound of the guy's apology.

'...so sorry, I didn't mean to scare you.' His voice was pleasantly rich, that warm woody tone that some Americans have. Sounded like a bass guitar, a good whisky, an autumn day. Sounded male.

'Am I late? I had a bit of trouble finding the place,' he continued, taking off his jacket and looking around for a chair to put it down. I was mildly confused by his actions, but still lost in that dizzy, detached space I get to when I'm painting, and mesmerised also by the sight of him. A tangle of tarry-black curls that was shockingly dark against his white skin. Those perfectly drawn lips, a full Cupid's bow as red as carmine that gave his face a cruel, tender beauty. His cheekbones sat high and proud. And the lines of his body – I could see even under the loose-fit trousers and shirt that he had a sculpted body. The way he moved. The way he stood, jacket in hand, letting the clothes hang from his bones with a silent confidence that suggested that underneath he was hard and perfect.

'Uh, are we working in here?' he asked, looking a little confused by my silence. I stared back, trying to figure it out. His lovely blue eyes narrowed.

'Jo?'

Then it clicked. 'Joe' worked next door. Big photo-realist charcoals. Young men, mostly. He hired models from time to time, had the poor bastards pose in the icy studio space for a tenner an hour. This guy was a stray. I opened my mouth, to laugh, to tell him his mistake. To point him in the direction of Joe's space.

Instead, I surprised myself. Perhaps the fumes had overcome me.

'Yeah.' I nodded. 'We're working in here.'

And that little white lie, I realised afterwards, was where I crossed the line. I'd stolen Joe's model. I was telling a stranger to strip for me. Strangely calm, but with a heart that was hammering like a drum, I watched as he moved across the space.

Remembering life-drawing etiquette, I shook myself pulled the curtain across the doorway, and ducked outside for a moment, It's fine to stare at the model while you're drawing them, but modesty forbids you watch them undress.

I left a chink. Enough to see my borrowed model unbutton his shirt and quickly, casually remove it. Skin like marble, firm and smooth. The form of him, the curves and the tense swell of his muscles. His low-slung trousers showed a pair of sharp hip bones, and I swallowed as he reached down to pop the button, unzip. He pulled down trousers and shorts in one movement, revealing the graceful legs of a dancer and the dark mess of his pubic hair. In the centre nested his long soft cock and the dusky-rose sac of his balls. I couldn't take my eyes off him. Watched his cock swing gently as he piled his clothes on the floor and stood waiting. Hugging himself, rubbing his arms to try and warm himself.

The studio temperature usually hovered around ten degrees – a fucking icebox no matter how warm it was outside.

Clearing my throat, I walked back in and started ferreting around for a sketchbook, a stick of charcoal.

'How do you want me?'

His question could have been entirely innocent, but as I looked at him standing there hugging himself, calmly displaying his full-frontal cock and balls, I thought I saw a faint spark in his expression. The slightest curl of his lip.

'*It only takes eye contact.*' I remembered Sandy's lesson on how to tumble a man.

'*A little smile. That's all. Then it's just a matter of finding out how to cross the distance between you and touch them.*'

Well, I couldn't just march up and grab him. No matter how strokable that gorgeous body looked, I had a charade to keep up.

'Uh, standing, is that OK? One hand on your shoulder, your weight on the right foot. Yeah, that's it.'

I couldn't help it, the way he looked. I couldn't resist recreating the pose of David, the classic stance. A tilt to the hips, the suggestion of vulnerability despite the strength of the body. I was playing with him. But he seemed willing to go along with it. He shifted and relaxed into the pose. He turned his face and showed the sweep of his neck. I could bite into that, I thought, imagining the smell of him – aftershave and soap and the sweet tang of male sweat.

I drew him slowly, pulling the charcoal over the paper like I was stroking the contours of his flesh. Smudging the lines with my finger, I had the sense of running my fingertip along his arm, across his abdomen, down his hipbone. His body hair was sparsely scattered – little tufts under his arms, a trail from his belly button spreading out over his groin. I worked deeper with the charcoal, enjoying the chance to ogle his cock. Keeping my face poker straight. Drinking in his beauty.

The Renaissance artists believed the study of the male form was the highest of arts. As I drew my model's beautiful form, I felt inclined to agree.

I was so absorbed by the task, it was only after half an hour that I noticed the shake in his legs.

'Oh Christ, sorry. Do you want a break?' I said.

He relaxed immediately, shaking his limbs out and slapping at his leg. 'Circulation's gone,' he said, rubbing vigorously.

The sound was like charcoal scribbling over paper, and it made me want to feel his hands on my body with the same friction.

'Pins and needles,' he said. 'Fuckin' cold in here, too.'

'I don't really notice it any more,' I said.

'No, you're totally absorbed. Can I have a look?'

I blushed. I actually blushed. Showing someone how you see them naked is a tricky moment. Still, I couldn't refuse. I stepped back, and let him walk round to see the sketches on the easel. Now we were close. The gap between us, as Sandy described it, was very small. I stood as still as I could. My hands were black with charcoal dust.

He nodded, and looked at me thoughtfully, like he was appraising me. 'Beautiful drawing. You have a mark –' He reached up to rub at my cheek. Let his thumb push down to my mouth. Held my chin and tilted my face up. Leant over, brought his face closer to mine, his eyes glittering and his mouth open, hot breath on my skin.

The distance reduced to zero and his mouth was on me, wet lips covering mine in a warm shock. All of a sudden the cold tension of the studio was flooded with sensation – the quiet northern light was eclipsed by the movement of this man against me, his hot human aliveness crashing into my world, encircling me, gripping

me in those naked marble-smooth arms. Everything was dark, but dark in the way of flesh, with
a heartbeat and a pulse and the vivid animal
sounds filling my ears.

I didn't pull away, and I didn't miss the smell
of love in the air. Instead, I felt the delicious
surprise of an unfamiliar man kissing me, and the
want and the need to feel him closer yet. Michel-
angelo always said the sculpture was already in
the stone, and he just had to work out how to find
it. When the model kissed me, it felt like he'd
found a new image of me, of what I could be. Like
he'd dug out the long-forgotten, reckless girl I used
to be from where she was buried deep in the cold
hard rock and brought me back to life.

His prick was stiffening, pressing against my
leg, while he slid his tongue into my mouth and
we tasted each other.

'*A mouthful of fun,*' Sandy had said.

I'd never been so hungry in my life. I knelt.

The wood planks of the studio floor were hard
under my knees as I took hold of the guy's hips
and pulled him towards me. I buried my face in
his pubic hair, letting it scratch against my mouth.
His cock bobbed against my cheek and I nuzzled
at it, feeling the smoothness and the heat of what
I'd been longing for for months. I'd spent a half-
hour looking at his body, trying to recreate it on
paper, but drawing his beauty was nowhere near
close enough to this. Touching him, taking him in
my mouth, sucking on him. Tasting the bitter-

sweet honey of his pre-cum as his cock swelled and grew rock hard.

Fuck drawing, I thought. It doesn't get to the heart of the matter. I realised just how flat a picture can be, as his hands tangled in my hair and I pulled at his ass, sticking a fingertip into his hole and feeling the corresponding spasm in his cock. This wasn't static, everything was in motion, stimulating all my senses at once, and we were sinking inside each other, intertwining, pushing and pulling at each other. He was tumbling down to kneel in front of me and his hands were burrowing into my clothes, seeking out the pockets of heat, the dark and wet spots that connected straight to my brain. His fingers ran into my knickers, slid quickly between my thighs and into my pussy. A slight resistance, before he found the groove and the moisture of my pussy and dived into it. Two fingers, three, jammed inside me, opening me up, wriggling in there with a funny little shock before I felt the rhythm of it, the to and fro rocking that made me feel like my body was caught in a tide. Waves ebbing and flowing, he was imitating the beat of sex that would sink into me and pull me under.

I couldn't even get my jeans off before he was pushing me over, holding his cock to guide it in and nudging at my slit.

'Stop, stop, wait,' I said, remembering one of Sandy's rules. 'We should use a condom.'

He nodded, breathless and beyond speaking

now, then leapt up nimbly to find his jeans and check the pockets. He sprinted back to where I lay with a foil square in his hand.

'You brought one to work?' I couldn't quite believe it. Was I the only person in Glasgow who didn't anticipate a casual fuck at lunchtime?

My model grinned, biting at the foil to rip it open. He had a wicked smile. 'Boy scout motto. Always "Be Prepared". You never know who you'll bump into.'

I wasn't in any position to argue, so I gave in and just marvelled at the sight of him, cock in hand, unrolling the rubber down his length and checking to see it was on tight. I lay back.

But he wasn't ready. The pause seemed to have given him an idea. 'How about we even the score a little?'

'How d'you mean?'

'You've spent half an hour staring at every inch of my naked ass. But I haven't even had a peek. I feel like I hardly know you.'

I laughed. It was a little one-sided − a fully clothed artist taking advantage of her new employee.

Even so, I felt strangely shy as I struggled out of my jeans and sweatshirt. Untying my shoelaces, I could feel his eyes on me, curious and searching. My skin seemed fragile, tender − as if it had never been exposed to daylight before. I was struck forcefully with the realisation of what I was doing − getting naked and amorous with a total stranger. I unhooked my bra and forced myself to resist the desire to cover my breasts. I slipped out of my panties and sat back while he looked at me.

The awareness of his gaze on my body had an unexpected effect. Even as my cheeks reddened with shame, I felt my spine arch, my hips rock a little. I was leaning back and enjoying this display, presenting my naked breasts to this man like a glamour model. My inner voice screamed '*Crazy*', but my body was opening to his attention. Then it dawned on me. I was showing off.

Why the hell not? What did I have to lose? I didn't even know this guy's name, and he'd probably disappear into the anonymous city in an hour or so. We were just having a brief taste of each other. A little adventure.

Suddenly reckless, I spread my legs for him in invitation. I was acting lewd, shocking myself, and I hadn't felt so damn alive in months. He swept down to join me, to kiss me again with those perfectly pretty lips and press the length of his body over mine. When his cock nudged at my slit and then entered me, it felt like I'd discovered the fast way to make a new friend. I don't mean that glibly either – he was moving in me so softly and so intensely I felt I was suddenly close to him, not just interlocked physically, but discovering him in a way that hours of late-night conversations and shy dates just wouldn't do. How else do you know a man, I thought, as his cock – long and thin and hard – filled me. I could feel him going deep and grinding against my pubic bone.

The quality of his love-making was as much part of him as his conversation – light and rapid, eager and somehow tender. He cradled my head with one hand to kiss me, lifting my mouth towards his. The kindness of strangers, I thought. He fucked me with easy strokes, and the rhythm I'd felt earlier – his hand inside me, darting against the inside of my cunt – was repeated with his hips. His kisses were playful and interspersed with little bites. As his hand roved down to stroke my body, he tweaked my nipples and gripped handfuls of flesh. He wormed his hand in between us, flicked at my clit, latched onto it and started frigging me in time with his fucking.

My body was opening up to him, hungry for the thump and bang of his hips against mine and eager to absorb his cock as deep as I could. We rolled on the floor, collecting broken bits of charcoal on our flesh and slipping on a pool of turpentine or oil or something, and the two of us kept sucking at each other, licking and thrusting and not giving a fuck how dirty and cold and uncomfortable our situation was. I had his hand hard against my clit now, and he was fucking me less playfully, driving into me with more emphatic pushes, pulling back as if he was taking a big in-breath, running his cock back into me with the urgency of approaching orgasm. I was jarred against the floor, hit hard by his body every time he pushed into me, feeling the magical tingling buzz in my cunt that meant I was going to come too, all over his hand and with him stuck deep and hard inside me all the way to the hilt. The whole of my body, inside and out, was alive and screaming for release, every part of me fucking back and forth, rubbing up against him, feeling him in and on and around me as he thrust with big heavy hip-jerks. It hit, hard.

He jolted against me one last time.

And cried out, and spilt himself inside me, and finally made my orgasm explode like a black starburst. Deep in my brain the inverse of colour swept through me, blanked out my mind, swallowed colour and transmuted it into pure burning, animal sensation.

Our bodies dissolved together and shook, hands slipping over each other, clutching hard, grunts and moans falling from our mouths involuntarily.

Perhaps I had lost my mind. I rolled around on the floor, feeling the last sweet stings of orgasm shoot through me, making me shiver as I held onto the guy.

I felt the sweat cool on my body almost instantly, the hard floor and the scratches on my ass and back from whatever the hell mess we'd just been lying on. The sudden emptiness as he pulled out of me, leaving my pussy tender, free-falling. The cold air rushing at my body, reality hardening the edges of the moment. Him sitting back and the unfamiliarity of his face reasserting itself. Looking shockingly strange. I didn't know him.

The distance between us was suddenly as great as it was when he'd first entered the studio – two strangers in daylight, trying to breathe normally.

There was an awkward moment when it came to paying him – and when I had to admit I'd nicked him from Joe's life-drawing session. But we laughed it off and, as he took his leave with a curiously chaste little kiss, I felt a sudden pang of affection for him. Not that we'd be repeating the encounter – that was pretty clear. After you've fucked someone on your studio floor without asking their name first, you'd be hard put to go through the whole rigmarole of dating and flirtation.

It was a short and sweet encounter, nothing more. But my heart felt somehow lighter that evening as I walked home with the rolled-up sketches under my arm and an aching body. I would pin up the pictures of my 'David' on my bedroom wall to remind me of my studio adventure. To show myself that beauty can turn up in unexpected places and that life tastes sweeter when you take the odd risk. I walked across town and for the first time in a year felt like I was plugged in to life. Part of the whole colourful, terrifying, electric game; like the switch my heart had been flicked to 'on' again.

In the swarming, messy crowds of rush hour I

saw the young guys and the rough-at-the-edges guys, dark and light and moving fast around me. A thousand possibilities for a little buzz, a little smile, a little warmth. A thousand gaps that weren't that hard to cross if you took the chance.

As Sandy says: 'There are a hundred kinds of love out there.'

Now I intend to taste as many as I can – one mouthful at a time.

Nikki Magennis is the author of the Black Lace novel *Circus Excite*

Public Relations
Mathilde Madden

Miles knows that Laura likes rope. Favours rope bondage above any other kind. Knots no boy scout knows and complicated diagrams, line drawings and photos that she insists Miles copy precisely on to her. Patterns and symbols like a new language. Written on the body.

Like a magic ritual, without the magic.

And after she has persuaded Miles to try every possible arrangement of jute and cotton and twine and her limbs on the ground, she starts talking about suspension. When Miles points out that his flat doesn't have the structure for that (and nor does hers) she tells him she knows the perfect place.

'Here, amongst all this ... this archive?' Miles stands in the basement of Laura's office building, drifting in an ocean of foolscap and filing drawers.

'Yes, look at the ceiling supports.'

Miles looks up. The ceiling is criss-crossed with metal supports. Above this basement there are four floors of Motif, the weighty PR company where Laura is an account manger. Maybe Motif needs all the extra reinforcement for all its wily, headline-grabbing schemes. Or maybe it was just designed by the god of kink to perfectly fulfil Laura's latest twisted desires.

Laura jumps up and catches one of the grid of iron beams, which supports the ceiling, swinging from it. 'It holds my weight, see, you don't need to worry.' While Miles watches she swings from beam to beam. Hand over hand. Monkeylike. Childlike. Un-Laura-like.

Miles looks around. The perfect place? Almost, but not quite. Not quite private enough, really. Oh, the building is empty right now, Miles is sure Laura wouldn't risk it otherwise. But he notices a small grimy window in the door to this storeroom and he notes it coolly like he does everything.

Casually, still on surveillance, Miles pulls open a filing drawer. It doesn't make a sound. Clearly Motif favours beautifully made expensive furniture – even in the basement. Miles lifts out a sheaf of paper. 'These files are ... these are personnel files. Aren't they confidential? This cabinet should be locked.'

'Yep. Whatever. Does it matter?' Laura drops the foot or so to the ground, landing clack-clack on her expensive stiletto heels. 'Anyway, shall we get on? I was thinking a Strappado.'

'I thought you wanted a suspension,' Miles says, not looking at her as he bends over to place the file he's holding down on the floor. Sitting on the floor next to it is a soft leather bag beside his.

A bag from which he starts to pull armfuls of bright-white cotton rope.

'I do,' Laura says, a little breathless already. As she speaks she clasps her hands behind her back and then slowly raises them up in the air, bending over automatically as she does so, until her arms are pointing straight up – perfectly vertical and rigid in the air – and her body is parallel to the floor. 'Strappado. Oh yes.'

Miles walks softly up behind her and presses his groin against her smoothly tailored buttocks, leaning across her back to place his lips right by her ear. Very slowly he whispers, 'A Strappado with suspension will dislocate both of your shoulders, you stupid little bitch.'

He knows that little note of hardness in his voice will have got to her. Somewhere inside. He also knows she won't show it. Yet.

But Laura gives him a little, because she catches her breath and wriggles against him, precise and calculated, turning her head so her eyes meet his. Too close to focus; black blurs. 'Just do it, Miles.'

Orders already is it? Silently, Miles straightens and catches Laura's patiently pre-positioned wrists in one hand, flicking the rope he is holding into place with the other; capturing them with bondage-master ease. He knows it feels like lovemaking to Laura when he wraps the ropes around her like this. More intimate than any caress. And he knows she's never known anyone who could give her what she needs – what she hates to admit she needs – like he can.

As Miles works on, throwing the end of the rope around the beam and securing it, Laura says nothing more that is intelligible apart from one single half-gasped 'God, tighter', as he clinches her elbows strictly behind her back.

But a few minutes later, after he's finally managed to re-tie the rope in a way that satisfies Laura's masochistic specifications, and is hitching off the one that holds her wrists high in the air, Laura looks over at him angrily, shuffling her feet. Feet that are still very much on the ground.

'This isn't a suspension.' Her angry lips barely move as she speaks.

Miles finishes tying off the rope and walks back to where she stands. She is bent right over by the way the rope is pulling her arms back and into the air. 'I know,' he says, 'I thought I'd take charge, make an executive decision.'

Her eyes are luminous. He particularly likes that. That fury. It's making him hard. 'But I said I wanted suspension. We came here for suspension.'

Miles smiles and doesn't reply. He has many possible replies in his head – mostly about doing what he wants for a change, or isn't he meant to be the one making the decisions here, or back to the old dislocation of shoulders idea. But he says nothing. Why explain? He knows he doesn't need to. He walks back to his old soft bag. He reaches inside and pulls out a spreader bar about three feet long, and with a lightly padded ankle cuff at each end. He carries it back over to Laura.

Quietly, he fastens each of her ankles to either

end of the bar, pulling her legs wide apart. Her feet are still on the floor though. Even with this extra stretch. This is not the suspension she wanted – but pretty uncomfortable nevertheless. Not giving Laura quite what she wants is always part of Miles's best and most deviously twisted plans. This position is every bit as frustrating as being suspended would be. Yet it's safe and restrictive and leaves Laura utterly vulnerable. It's also on Miles's terms. Laura growls low with annoyance, twisting pointlessly.

Miles stands up from where he was checking the ankle cuffs and looks at her for a moment, bending a little to get at eye level and then raising her defiant chin with his index finger.

He scrutinises her eyes. Was she there yet? Every time the same – she basically has to be forced into subspace, fighting tooth and claw all the damn way.

But yes, close now. Her eyes *are* a little glassy. The spreader bar has helped somewhat and in spite of herself she is going under. She is acquiescing. *Finally.*

And Miles smiles. 'You know, you'll enjoy it much more if you just let me do it. I thought you were supposed to be the submissive. How about submitting now and again?' He bends down and gets kiss-close to her lips. 'Or just shutting up?'

She growls again, pulling a little more defiance from somewhere. 'Make me.' She is practically dripping with it, but she doesn't fool Miles. He knows for certain now she is less than a breath away from sub-space. Well, maybe not a breath, maybe something a little more substantial.

Miles has the very thing to tip her over. 'Make you? Oh my pleasure.' He reaches in his pocket and pulls out a ball gag. Holding it up so she could see exactly what it is. Just a rubber ball on leather thong – the exact same thing she has seen a million times before – except that with this one the ball, which is usually red rubber, is sugar pink. Miles had been unable to resist it. Too perfect for her.

Laura looks at the gag and there's a second's delay, as if she's processing the information. 'How many times Miles,' she says eventually, 'how many times do I have to tell you I don't like being gagged?'

Miles's next smile is the one he knows is slow and seductive. Melting. 'Oh, you know I have such a terrible memory,' he says walking slowly towards where she is trussed and helpless, twisting, with her feet scuffling on the polished concrete floor.

'You try it and I'll safe word so fast –' But it's an empty threat.

'No. No you won't,' Miles interrupts and, holding her head still with a hasty handful of hair, he pushes the ball into her mouth. If she has any further complaints about Miles's treatment he's happily ignorant about them now.

Once the thong is tied tightly behind her head and her hair lovingly rearranged, Miles takes a step back. 'You never safe word, sweetheart, you know that,' he says. Then he leans in to peck her on the cheek and whispers, 'And pink is *so* your colour.'

The noises Laura makes after that are pretty loud, but unintelligible, so Miles simply tunes them out. He walks around her a couple of times and then stops behind her and drops his trousers.

He puts his hands on her hips to still her where she is struggling and squirming. He knows all his knots would hold through any amount of fighting, but he would still rather she calmed down so he could enjoy his handiwork. He slips a hand up her softly expensive skirt and she seems to respond then, moving into his touch. Wanting.

There's no underwear beneath her skirt and she's easily wet enough that he can tell he isn't going to have to bother with any kind of foreplay or lube. He takes his hand away, leaves a beat for her anticipation to build – wait for it – and then he slides inside.

He fucks her very, very gently, rocking on the balls of his feet. He knows what she would be expecting – wanting – at this point: rough treatment. A harsh nasty fucking; leaving her bruised and rope burnt. *Well, guess what you're not getting, baby?*

How long is it going to take her to realise that what he really relishes giving her is a sweet combination of exactly what she wants spiked with just enough of what she doesn't want to give him that feeling of controlling her? Controlling

Miss Uncontrollable. For him that's what it's all about.

He keeps his movements light and gentle because he doesn't want her to have a chance of coming. He knows how much that will drive her mad after the planning she's put into this.

But he does give her a little bit of something special. 'You know,' he breathes into her ear, pressing his chest down across her back and twisting around her bound arms, 'I've been thinking, all the time we've been here, about how much fun it would be to leave you like this.'

Laura makes a muffled sound, a moan that could be anything from desperate arousal to frustrated rage.

'Mmm-hmm. It would be so easy. At your place of work. And who'd find you? A cleaner? A boss? A good-looking co-worker? Would they cut you down? Maybe I could leave a sign on your arse, here, inviting anyone who found you to use you for their pleasure.'

Laura's moans get more intense and unreadable than ever. She's moving against him as far has her bondage will allow, but Miles keeps his movements as restrained as she is.

'It would be terrible for you,' Miles continues, 'to be exposed like that. I know you like to keep this wanton side of yourself very private. Ice queen in public, bitch on heat in private. Oh, I know the drill. Ironic, isn't it that you work in public relations, when you like your own relations to be kept so very private.'

Laura moans. She's close to coming. Miles stops talking then. Laura still has a long time to wait before that. And then, when she is standing growling and spluttering frustratedly into his pink gag, with his warm semen gliding down her glass-smooth stockings, he walks away from her, retrieves the files he had slipped into his bag and begins to read.

Her file and Gabriel Blaine's.

It's nearly an hour later when he lets her go. He's found a lot more information in the forgotten drawers of Motif's basement since then. Including the time the late-night cleaners start their shift. Miles spotted the cleaning supplies storeroom next to the basement when they came in and decides to sit tight for the shift starting. He wonders if any of the cleaners look through the base-ment window as they collect their buckets and baskets of spray cans. He waits until he has lis-tened to them come and go and confused panic lights Laura's eyes.

'I am never playing with you again,' Laura spits as he unhitches the rope that supports her, letting her stiff limbs tumble to the floor.

'Oh, don't pretend you didn't love every min-ute,' he says, straddling her as she lies on the floor and tugging loose the knots which hold her wrists.

And then, with her wrists mostly loose but still half-tangled in bits of rope and with the spreader bar still holding her ankles apart, Miles pushes her skirt up and presses his tongue against her wet cunt. She bucks. Fire in his hands. He can't resist pulling away and saying, 'So, you hated every minute, did you?'

'Uh.' Just a desperate noise.

He gives her back his tongue, twirling it around her clit until she screams so loudly that he swears he hears one of the cleaners knock over their bucket upstairs.

Before Laura has recovered, Miles has sorted and stowed all his rope and equipment back in his bag. Along with a couple of Motif's badly stored personnel files.

Later, very late at night, waiting for her to call, Miles flicks open Gabriel Blaine's file. The picture of him on the very first page had already told Miles all he needed to know when he looked at it in the basement. Dark hair, dark smile. This is the guy Laura is thinking of cheating on me with? Miles knows she has been thinking about it for at least a month.

Did you really think I wouldn't notice? Did she really think that, when she had had that expensive haircut, changed her make-up and started dropping a rather distinctive-sounding name into conversation just a little bit *too* often, a man like Miles wouldn't notice?

As he reads through Gabriel's file again, checks the dates, Miles notes that Gabriel started as account manager at Motif just over a month ago. How very unsurprising.

In some ways Miles thinks it's kind of sad. Sad

that a sparklingly intelligent woman like Laura could have her head turned by a walking, talking piece of beefcake like Gabriel Blaine, without really knowing if he could meet her very precise sexual needs.

Miles thinks about her then, semi-suspended from the ceiling in Motif's basement, twisting and making muffled noises into the pretty pink gag. Thinks about how wet she was when he fucked her, and how much wetter she was later when he pressed his mouth to her cunt. Wet and angry; always her way. Precise needs, indeed.

But the thing about needs like Laura's – or, indeed, needs like Miles's – is that they couldn't be met by just anyone. Laura needs to understand that. Finding someone who has it in them, who can climb and soar the way she needs them to, isn't something that she can tell by looking.

What people show in public, the way they present themselves to the world, often gives away nothing at all about what they want in bed. In fact, more often than not it's just the opposite. The powerful politician who wants to be tied up and whipped might be a cliché. But it's a cliché Miles has seen walking, talking and moaning with pleasure more times than he can count during his voyages through the sexual underworld.

Just a glance at Gabriel's photograph is enough for Miles to know that is how Laura sees him, though. All that packed muscle and that dark brooding brow.

Miles knows that, when Laura looks at Gabriel,

she imagines him slamming her up against the wall, kicking her legs apart, taking her hard, being the brutal beast he looks like. She sees a man who is all built – practically made of coiled power – and thinks that power just can't wait to be unleashed. It doesn't occur to her that it would be far more fitting to see all that urgent muscle bound and contained.

Because Miles knows what makes Gabriel tick. Not from looking at his public corporate face. Miles knows because Miles has met Gabriel before.

It was at a party. Some night after a club at some anonymous suburban house. Miles was there with a pretty girl on a dog leash whose name and face are now buried by their many successors. Thinking about it now, Miles finds that a bit shameful, but, in some ways, maybe that's what happens when you find the one – all the others are eclipsed by the blinding light, drowned out by the choirs of angels. Not that he thinks of Laura like that. Not really.

But, the party. Gabriel. He remembers Gabriel. Too pretty to go unnoticed. That great hulk was kneeling, handcuffed, kissing the boots of his mistress – or at least his mistress for the night.

Lots of people looked at Gabriel at that party. Even in a room full of tousled blondes badly packed into PVC, Gabriel, with his luminescent dark skin and his big bright eyes, drew the gazes like nothing else in the room. There is something about a big alpha-looking man on his knees that appeals to almost anyone. Miles watched Gabriel for a long time at that party, with the kind of detached fascination he had perfected for events like these. He watched for far longer than he should have done to be fair to his own pretty thing.

He was watching when the seated mistress had lifted her foot from the floor, so Gabriel could bend right down and suck on her stiletto heel like it was a slender cock. And he watched Gabriel's own cock – heavy, hard and barely contained by the white jock he was wearing – twitch and throb as she forced the shaft in and out of his lips.

So Miles knows that when Gabriel looks at Laura he doesn't see what she hopes he sees. He doesn't think about what a delicious sight she'll be, brought down a peg or two, with all the puff taken out of her billowing sails. Oh no. He doesn't see Laura the way Miles sees her. Miles knows that when Gabriel looks at Laura his cock gets hard imagining how that strict, sharp-tongued bitch she presents in the boardroom at Motif would translate her nasty act to his bedroom. And to him, helpless and tormented beneath her sharp heels.

Those higher-than-high heels – the conundrum they embody. Miles knows that Gabriel must think of them as signals of Laura's taste for cruel dominance – pedestals – but he knows that they are really a part of her twisted masochism.

So there's poor Gabriel; like Laura just too young and pretty to realise that a woman who struts like a dominatrix in public might be something rather different between the rubber sheets.

It's while Miles is thinking about this that he notices that Laura still hasn't called. He torments himself by thinking that she's at home, fantasising about Gabriel.

He looks over at Laura's file – he'd taken that from Motif's basement too. He notices her date of birth and he gets an idea. Wouldn't Gabriel Blaine be a perfect way to give Laura exactly what she wanted in exactly the way she didn't want it?

The next morning, Miles calls Gabriel at Motif. He pretends to be talking business for a while, saying he has a new company and needs a public-relations firm. Then he says, 'Your name is familiar, though, Gabriel Blaine?'

Gabriel laughs. A deep boom of a laugh. Miles imagines Laura, sitting only feet away, squeezing her thighs together at that dark sound, casting it as potentially a laugh of sadistic glee. 'It's a name people tend to remember,' Gabriel says.

'Oh, I know,' says Miles. 'But where do I know you from? Hang on ... Are you a friend of Sabrina?'

'Sabrina?' Gabriel says, the tiniest hitch in his voice.

'Mmm, you know who I mean, don't you?'

'Yes.'

Sabrina is the name of the dominatrix Miles

saw Gabriel with at that party. He isn't really up on that kind of thing, but he called around. Finally found someone who remembered that party better than he did. Remembered Gabriel. Remembered who he was with.

It isn't about blackmail with Miles, it's about persuasion. Miles likes being persuasive. Actually revels in it. And Gabriel turns out to be the kind of man who is easily persuaded by the right kind of invitation.

Laura calls Miles in the end. She always does. She let it go a week this time, which was almost her record, but then, one hot night . . .

'Hey, Miles. It's Laura.'

'Laura . . .? I don't . . .?'

'Oh fuck off, Miles, don't give me that fake Laura-who crap. I want to meet up.'

'Oh. *That* Laura.'

'Listen, I was thinking, it's my birthday next week. How about we do something special? I was thinking something long term. Over the whole weekend. A captivity scene. We'd need equipment, but I can go online. Get some new stuff. Maybe metal.'

'Metal, that's new for you. I thought you were all about rope?'

'I can change my mind, can't I?'

'Yeah, OK,' Miles says, trying not to chuckle because, really, this is just too perfect.

'Great!' Laura sounds almost surprised that he agrees to what she wants so easily. But she doesn't sound wary. Even now, Laura still doesn't seem to check for a catch. 'Shall I go online, order some stuff?'

'No, baby, leave it to me.'

Miles knows that Laura is being impulsive again. Asking for the moon. He knows that the kind of custom-made hardcore metal restraints she's thinking of are crazy expensive and would take months to be delivered if ordered online. But Miles knows about the Mole's House.

Tinkle-tinkle.

'Ah, hello, sir. No lady friend?' The Mole is brisk and small with dark tight eyes like bugle beads. He sits behind the counter working on a wide strip of black leather with a knife easily the length of his own forearm.

'No. Not today.' Miles wonders which lady he's referring to. When had he last been here? Like most of his people he bought so many toys online these days.

'Ah, that's quite the shame, sir.' The Mole glances down, gouges heavily with his knife twice, and then continues, 'So are you still interested in the percussion section?' He gestures towards a wall hung with canes, whips, paddles and crops, and one long bullwhip snaking across the top.

Miles shakes his head. 'No, not today.' He remembers then, the last time. A thin blonde, crazy as a masochist; she was always dragging him here for new toys to hit her with.

But that isn't the requirement today. Today Miles wants restraints. Just as Laura had outlined. Metal. Strong ones. Big ones. Not the cheap leather or tinny handcuffs he knows he would be offered in the normal sexual recreation shops in Soho. And not the single old set of metal handcuffs he has back at home.

Gabriel is a big man. Miles remembers that party again, how Gabriel's thick wrists looked cartoonish in a pair of thin handcuffs. Miles wants the aesthetic to be right. And he wants stuff he can depend on. He needs the Mole's House.

The Mole frowns when he explains what he needs.

'These are very big measurements,' he says in an accent Miles can't place and isn't even sure is real.

Miles nods. He sees the look in the Mole's eyes and decides to let him wonder.

The Mole looks at Miles for a moment more, his little nose wrinkling and his whiskers – because at that moment he really did seem to have whiskers – shaking with a rhythm all of their own. And then he says, 'I think you should step out back, sir.'

The Mole leads the way through a rattling beaded curtain and into a room that is even darker and more groaningly ominous than the shop proper. The room is full of furniture. 'Alternative' furniture.

The shuffling Mole walks over to a wall where a mass of chains, rings, hooks and manacles are tangled and draped together, swooping off ceiling hooks and dangling like forest branches. But as the Mole turns, weighing a great iron ring in his hands and grinning toothily, Miles sees the cage and his idea ratchets up a level.

On Friday evening, Miles picks Laura up. He notices that she is wearing a black dress, which he has often said that he liked, but when she gets into the car he doesn't say anything. Not even 'Happy birthday'.

Laura isn't so quiet. She's full of questions, curiosity, demands. 'You got them, right? Metal restraints. I took Monday off work just in case. I mean, Gabriel can cope without me.'

'I'm sure Gabriel can cope,' Miles says, stressing almost every word in the sentence.

'OK, so what's the plan? You're going to chain me up, what, standing?'

'Why don't you just wait and see?'

'I hate "wait and see". I want to *know*. *Now*. How do I know that it's something I'll like?'

'Laura, baby. You'll love it. I promise. It's exactly what you want.'

'Oh really? You know exactly what I want now, do you?'

'Oh yeah.' *And I'm going to give it to you.*

Laura bounces up the steps ahead of Miles – his flat is on the third floor. Her excitement is making him feel a little strange. Torn between a desire to turn this all around and give her what she wants and a deep pulse in his cock when he thinks about how twisted everything is going to become when he opens the door.

He arrives at the door to his flat with Laura waiting, hopping from foot to stilettoed foot. Eager. Buzzing. He puts his key in the lock and stands back to let her enter first.

She heads straight in the living room. Probably hoping that's where her new toys will be. Hoping right. Over the clatter of his keys on the hall table he hears her say, 'Oh, why have you got the curtains closed in here?' And then, 'What *is* this?' And then, 'God. What the . . . Oh my God! Gabriel?'

Miles moves to the living-room doorway so he can see her. See her face when she sees her gift – exactly what she wants and yet, not what she wants at all. Gabriel Blaine, her big hard-bodied fantasy dom, trussed in metal manacles and crouching in a cage Miles bought from the Mole's House. The cage isn't that small, but Gabriel is so big that his body inside the cage looks like an optical illusion. His muscles are burnished with sweat as he struggles and shifts position constantly in the small space. He's crouched, his big haunches splayed by his curled chest. His head bowed by the top of the cage. His hands are chained behind his back. His ankles are cuffed together too – albeit rather needlessly. He's naked, but a little scrap of metal glints at his crotch. An impulse buy.

Laura's expression won't stay still. She's shocked, horrified, aroused, confused . . .

Aroused?

Miles never saw that coming.

'Laura?' he says.

Laura turns and pushes past him into the hallway. For a moment Miles thinks she's leaving. Walking out. But she stops by the hall table and picks up Miles's keys. A set of keys that contains a few extra ones tonight. The keys to Gabriel's restraints.

She pockets them and heads back into the living room, pausing only to close the door softly in Miles's face.

Miles is sitting out in the hall, listening to the sounds coming from behind the closed door – familiar sounds of two people making each other very, very happy. He thinks how funny it is that just as what a person shows you in public can hide what they are really like in private, what they show you in private can sometimes be just another mask. Like peeling an onion. Who'd have thought that Laura would pull a switch on him like that?

Just goes to show, you never can tell.

Mathilde Madden is the author of the Black Lace novels *Mad About the Boy*, *Peep Show* and *Equal Opportunities*.

Pickup Girl A. D. R. Forte

It's that truck he has. That big, shiny metal and chrome monstrosity that purrs in diesel double-bass. It's a country-boy cowboy truck: dooley, off-road tyres, toolbox, even hunting lights. I've seen plenty like it around here and I know the type that drives them. Only thing is, he ain't a cowboy; not in the least, most generous stretch of the imagination. And maybe that's why.

Why I want him to drive me out into the warm wistful night of a Texan summer. Speed down an empty country road and turn off into a deserted field where only the stars watch. And there under the starlight, surrounded by nothing but night and open space, fuck me good and hard in the bed of that truck in true cowboy style.

Problem is, he wouldn't dare.

I know few people who make such a point of playing by the rules as Nathaniel David Marble. He's always on time. He always knows what to say. And his khakis never have a wrinkle. Sometimes I think his pants must be bewitched, goodness knows I find myself staring at them often enough, wishing they would just disappear.

I know it probably doesn't improve his opinion of me when I give in to sudden random fits of laughter, but it would probably be much worse if he knew I was picturing a band of twinkling, enchanted stars encircling his abruptly bare hard-on. Before I got down on my knees and started sucking him off with no regard to time or place or decent behaviour. I think the knowledge of that little fantasy would be more than he could handle.

Or maybe not. After all, he bought that damned truck. Tony, my stylist and self-proclaimed expert on men of any orientation, would say he's compensating. But I venture to disagree. A man who's compensating doesn't have quiet confidence. He doesn't move through life with the air that he owns the world and never feels compelled to prove it. A man who doesn't have self-esteem doesn't have near-inhuman self-control.

Sure, he doesn't fuck casual acquaintances. Flirting isn't in his vocabulary. Yet, even so, I've caught a stray glance or a treacherous smile from time to time. And, even fewer and further between, I've brushed up against a temper simmering beneath that cool façade. I've faced Nate Marble down before and I've liked it. I'd like it even more if I had him twisting and arching under me, begging me to ride him harder. If only. But maybe ... maybe he just needs direction.

I park my truck next to his. He knows it's mine and he'll know the black sandals and the suede bag on the passenger seat are mine. An edge of navy lace and silk peeks out of the open flap of the bag, part of some unknown garment. The sandals are black patent leather, four-inch heels.

Let his imagination come up with the reason for why they're tossed so carelessly when he knows I'm fanatically neat, neater than he is. Let his fantasy conjure up the picture of me wearing them and that lacy, silky something. I wonder what he'll think of, wonder what effect it'll have. There's a lot I would give to know. I'm grinning as I lock the door and leave the parking garage.

The next day I catch him looking at me despite his best pretence to be absorbed in the contents of the folder in his hand. So of course I walk right up to him.

'Hey, Nate.'

'Hi,' he replies, looking straight up and making eye contact. Sassy bastard.

'I didn't know you'd got a new truck.'

He starts to explain, to say something about when or where that I don't care about.

'I really like it.'

That cuts him off and the faintest trace of pink crosses his cheeks.

Embarrassment or pleasure?

'Thanks.'

He flips the folder closed and smiles. Not his polite smile – this smile reaches all the way to his clever, dark eyes, that are the colour of polished oak. Those eyes that have passed me over with cool indifference and blazed at me with impatience before. Today he cannot or will not look away, and the spark in his gaze is neither disgust nor anger.

'Take me for a ride in it sometime, OK?' I say as I smile and give his arm the lightest of squeezes. Then I walk away as if the whole conversation was just my attempt at being polite. As if I didn't really care. Oh, but I saw his face as I released his arm. Blazing red.

He comes to find me when the afternoon shadows lie in charcoal chunks and squares like giant tyre treads over my desk. He stands in the doorway and looks me over, weighing the plus-deltas. Doesn't he know that just by being there he's already sealed his fate?

Might be tonight, or next week, or six months from now. But he's as good as roped and hog-tied. He asks how my last meeting went. And I tell him 'great' and ask what's up. Why is he here? He tries to make up an answer, fumbles over it and gives in. Shrugs. He just came by to say hello.

I throw my head back and laugh and he stares at me, silent and smiling a secret smile as if to suggest he knows something I don't.

Oh, sweetheart, you don't know a thing. Pretend all you want that this is not what it seems. You came to me. You're already mine.

We have a trip to a remote office. It's no coincidence that we elect to sync up responsibilities at that site on the same week. But he stops in twice at my office to mention that it 'really is a neat coincidence how that worked out'. Well. If it makes him feel better. I've got time for as long as he wants to play this game.

Oh, sweetheart, don't you know the waiting makes it hotter – so much hotter?

Goddamned hot. Desert heat the moment we step through the airport sliding glass doors onto baking-stone concrete and steaming blacktop. Heat that shimmers and moves on the executive taxis and stretch limos and beat-up four-doors crowding the concourse like a living, liquid thing. And the rental car doesn't fit either of us.

Yeah, there's plenty of room. But, by getting into that mulberry-coloured full-size sedan, we leave something else outside. We fit the image suddenly, and in those moments where we're reminded of who we ought to be, how we ought to behave, we don't know what to do.

I look out the window and fiddle with the air vent and my billfold while he adjusts the seat, the steering, turns up the air to an icy blast. And then I bless my carry-on bag as it falls over in the back seat. I lean back to shove it into place and my skirt slides up over the edges of my stockings.

I'm wearing stay-ups. Forget the garters. That strip of perfectly bare skin between French lace and cotton polyester promises that there's nothing else. No impediment of buttons or cloth to make fingers pause and fumble. Nothing to slow his speed.

He's turned to look at me, one hand on the

steering wheel, one hand on the gear shift. His lips are parted. Only when he realises a full three slow seconds have gone by and I'm doing nothing but looking at him with my eyebrows raised does he clamp them shut firmly. Refusal.

'Everything OK?' he asks.

I smile. Such control, my gorgeous Nate.

'Just peachy,' I say.

I wriggle back into place and make a token effort at pulling my skirt back down. It's not my fault if I can't get the hem quite back down to my knee – I've got my seatbelt on. I mean, really, how much squirming around can I possibly do in the interests of modesty? But he's got all his attention fixed on the road, not even sparing a glance my way. Iron-clad control. And by the time we hit the freeway he's doing nearly eighty.

I don't know how we get lost. But at some point I look out at the miles of sand and wind-stripped rock stretching out behind the telephone poles on either side of the road and realise we're nowhere near civilisation. I see him glance at the GPS console that confidently lets us know we're fifty miles north of the city. Never mind that we took the southbound freeway from the airport.

With an irritated grumble, he turns the console off.

'Well, this is fun.'

'Is it?' I put my notebook down and turn to him. I stick the end of my pen between my teeth and give him a considering look. 'I don't know about you but I could think of a lot more fun things than being lost in the back of nowhere.'

I tap the pen on my lips in mock thoughtful fashion until he gives in and laughs.

'I wonder what you'd consider fun.' He glances at me from the corner of his eyes and I pretend the question is as innocent as the tone it's delivered in.

'Right about now, a drink. Preferably with alcohol, but we'll take what we can get.'

I point ahead with the pen. The two lanes of the road have narrowed, with packed dust replacing what was paved shoulder ten miles back. Dust billows across the road and the distance shimmers behind a quicksilver curtain of heat, but out of the haze before us rise the ubiquitous white numerals of a gas-station sign.

'And maybe you can ask for directions.'

He gives me a look that could shred leather and I dissolve in laughter. The upholstery of the car seat is rough against the skin of my thighs where my skirt is well above my stockings, and, even on full blast, the air conditioning suddenly seems inadequate. First I think it's a blessing this material doesn't wrinkle much because my skirt is a hopeless crumple. And, second, that if I had my way it would be getting a helluva lot more crumpled right now. The sound of his voice at that moment feels like a hand sliding deftly between skin and cloth.

'Might as well get gas too since . . .'

It's hard as hell to keep up a façade of nonchalance right then, to manage a cool, smart-ass remark. But somehow I do, interrupting him mid-sentence.

'Since you might not be able to find the way back ever?'

We're parked at the single pump in what passes for a paved lot, although the desert is doing its best to reclaim the spot with the relentless scrubbing of sand and wind. A handwritten cardboard sign on the pump proclaims 'CASH/CHECK PAY INSIDE STORE FIRST!' I guess by that that it means the formerly whitewashed building sitting another thirty feet back from the pump and guarded by an ice freezer and a warped-iron bench outside. There's not a soul in sight.

He pauses in the act of getting out of the car and looks back. The pale-blue and white linen of his shirt is pulled tight across his shoulder. I should reach out and stroke the hard curve of muscle underneath, run my fingers up the back of his neck.

'You're asking for it,' he says, with a smile.

'Asking for what?' I want to goad him over that line, make him abandon propriety first.

'It.'

He's already out of the car.

Now it's my turn to feel my face burn. OK, sweetheart, so I underestimated you. You're playing with me too.

But I've got no problem throwing my hand.

Feeling silly, I grin anyway as I exit the car and walk towards the neon lottery sign struggling to make itself seen through a grimy windowpane. It doesn't matter how this plays out. Either way, I still win.

The 'store' is scarcely more than four sagging walls and a roof held together with a wish and a prayer. A rusty bell wrapped around the door handle with a length of wire jangles in fabulous discordance as I enter. At least the inside has the decency to boast a single humming refrigerator crammed into one corner. I head towards it with a nod to the ancient clerk sitting at the counter and half-snoozing over his porno mag.

There are plenty more where his came from under the dirty glass counter top. As I set bottles of wonderfully cold soda down on the counter I look the magazines over and contemplate getting one. Take it back to the car and tell Nate it's reading material for when I'm at the hotel.

I laugh aloud and the clerk wakes up abruptly, sending the magazine slithering off his lap.

It lands on the floor and flips open to reveal a blonde vixen in a fascinating pose involving two pillows, a table and an amazing sense of balance. I wonder if Nate would enjoy me like that, all pink and white lace and diamond-shimmer glossy lips. I can almost feel the pillows yielding to my weight, feel Nate's hands ...

The clerk grunts and gives me a contemptuous look, then bends to pick up the magazine with a mumbled apology. Evidently, he's mistaken my riveted fascination with the picture for embarrassment or outrage.

'No. It's OK really,' I mumble back, handing over my credit card. I'm amazed they even have a credit card machine in this place. As I wait the interminable age for the clerk to punch in the numbers with silver-ringed, wrinkled brown fingers, and then another aeon for the charge to authorise, my mind races.

I could ask for directions, but I don't want to know where we are. I don't want a set of clearly defined, helpful instructions on how to get to civilisation at eighty miles an hour. I'm right where I wanted to be: in the middle of nowhere, with him and only a couple thousand pounds of sheet metal and an engine to return us to sanity. When we want to return. If we want to.

I scribble my name on the credit-card slip and pick up the bottles with an absent-minded word of thanks to the clerk. He nods and shuffles away to disappear behind a bead curtain at the back of the store. It's like he's gone offstage intentionally, left me with free reign to do what I will.

Hot air rises up in a wave as I push the door open and, bottles in one hand, clumsily, nervously unbutton the top of my shirt. Two buttons only, just enough and not too much. I shake my hair back out of the way and head for the car – no, I *stalk* my way back to the car.

I've made up my mind. Here. And now.

* * *

The nozzle is still in the gas tank and he's leaning against the car looking at the map from the rental company.

He looks up and meets my gaze full on, and his eyebrows lift ever so slightly.

'So I think I know where we are now,' he says.

'Yeah? Well, good,' I reply in a tone that says I don't give a shit.

I step over the pump hose slowly, pausing an extra half-heartbeat with one leg on either side, straddling the hose. Then I swing the other leg over. The movement puts me less than a foot from his chest. He breathes out slowly, steadily, looking at me with those marvellous eyes.

Dark eyes, dark hair. I notice his shirt sleeves are folded back once, baring his arms almost to the elbows. Damn. Give him a couple days in this desert sun and that golden-toned skin will darken to copper. I picture him: no shirt, jeans, headband, leaning against that cowboy truck of his and watching me just like he's watching me now. Willing me to come hither.

I've opened my own drink on the way to the car and I take a long sip from it now, tilting my head back and letting the condensation drip from the bottle on to the front of my white linen shirt. He makes a soft sound and reaches for the unopened bottle in my left hand. But, before his fingers can touch it, I whisk it from his grasp.

I swallow my own sip and smile, and then lean into him, chest to chest. Reaching behind him, I balance the second bottle on the top of the car, and then inch closer so that this time my legs straddle his. With one hand braced on the car doorframe and my Mary Jane pumps on either side of his loafers, I hold him captive. I bring my bottle to his mouth and brush the plastic edge along his lips.

'Uh-uh.' I pull the bottle back a little. 'Work for it.'

He looks at me and shakes his head, as if to say 'no way is she really doing this'. But his cheeks are flushed with more than the heat, and he obeys. And I get to see just what kind of knowledge prissy, perfect, good-boy Nate really has.

His tongue circles the rim of the bottle where my lips have been just a minute before. He licks each ridge where the cap screws on with the tip. His tongue darts into the mouth of the bottle and moves in sinuous, twisted precision. When he closes his eyes I feel the vibration of his chest-deep moan all the way through the bottle and into my hand. All the way into my skin. I stare in amazed, confused desire at the motion of his lips and his tongue on the clear plastic, and my pulse beats in matching harmony.

I'm still mesmerised, helpless like a charmed snake, when he lifts his mouth from the bottle and turns. When he proceeds to do to my mouth what he's just finished showing me he can. But there's so much more you can do with hot, resilient flesh than with plastic. And I'm a quick learner.

Be careful when you charm a snake. After the spell's over, she's a thousand times more vicious.

When we end that kiss I'm surprised we haven't created enough static electricity to set the pump on fire. But his pretty lips are bruised now, and I know for a fact that the truck wasn't compensating for anything.

Somehow I've managed not to drop the soda bottle through all this. I remember it when his hand closes over mine and he raises the bottle. My fingers slide through his and I let him have it. I've got better things to do with my hands while he's occupied. There's a certain fantasy I've wanted to fulfil for a long, long time.

I unbuckle his belt, and then the buttons on his no-longer perfectly pressed khakis. Smiling, I run my hands along his legs as I sink downwards.

'Oh hell!' he says, half laughing.

'Oh hell, yeah,' I correct him. He's still got the map in his other hand and I grab it, neatly sliding it into place beneath my knees and the rough concrete. It's far from an ideal solution, but then I pull down his khakis and boxers, and I'm totally distracted again. I think I've never seen a man look so utterly at ease with his pants and underwear around his ankles. He sips his soda pop and smiles.

'Don't tell me you're intimidated.'

I snort. 'Intimidated my ass.'

My voice gets softer and my fingers circle his cock, teasing. 'Impressed is more like it. But...' I let my tongue flicker along the underside of his length and just over the tip. He sucks in his breath.

'I can more than handle you ...'

I spiral my tongue down his cock, almost enclosing him with my mouth – but not quite – and I feel his posture change, his body stiffen. I draw back and look up. At the naked, waiting lust in his face, my heart does a double flip. I love seeing that look, knowing it's all me. I close my teeth on the inner muscle at the top of his thigh, slowly, slowly add pressure until he groans aloud – a breathy, pleading, bite-me-harder-babe groan.

'... cowboy.'

I love the taste of him, the smell of him, the feel of him all the way into the back of my throat. There's nothing sexier than sucking a gorgeous guy off. The thought that it's nothing you should be doing anyway, that if Grandma saw you she'd faint, that it's damn hard to do on top of everything else, make it the hottest sexual act in the book. In any book.

And here on my knees at a gas-station pump in full view of the road and the whole damned world. With the smell of road dust and gasoline and engine oil in my nose; the hot metal of the car under my palms. With Nate – repressed, corporate, closet-cowboy Nate – moaning my name and fucking my mouth like it's the hottest piece of ass he's ever had. Yeah, this definitely counts as a Category 5 on the F-scale.

I'm torn between wanting to suck him until he comes and the slippery, aching friction between my legs. He makes the decision for me: his fingers tighten in my hair and he pushes me back. I lick my lips and stare at him hungrily, half displeased at having my pleasure taken away, half wild with lust.

'Up.'

I stand and he moves around behind me, sandwiching my body between his and the car. He lifts my arms and begins to unbutton the rest of my shirt. His breath is like the touch of a brand on my neck, but his hands are unhurried, confident, sensual. He unhooks my bra. I hold my breath. He slides bra and shirt off my shoulders, halfway down my arms. I release my breath and gasp for another as his palms retrace their path up over my skin. By the time his knuckles graze my nipples I'm dizzy.

And still his hands don't stop. Now their path travels down to my long-suffering skirt, raising it, crumpling it delightfully over my hips as he nudges me forward. My breasts brush hot maroon chrome and steel and I gasp and arch, pushing my bare ass right up against his cock.

He stills and I glance over my shoulder, meet eyes full of concern.

'You OK?'

I can't answer, I just nod and plead with my gaze for him to keep going. Impulsively, he kisses my mouth again, softer than before, so soft you'd think we were making love instead of fucking. He circles his left arm around me and pulls my back into the curve of his torso, holding me where he can kiss me to his heart's content. But his other hand is busy between my spread legs. And he kisses me like a lover all the while he fingers me like a whore.

But, when the first sweet, intense bubble of pleasure rises in my clit and courses through every muscle from my hips right down to my toes, I have to tear my mouth away for air. His fingers never stop. And, bereft of my lips, he turns his passion to my neck and my shoulder, his teeth nipping the naked skin. Each bite a tiny, incredible torture.

But it's still not enough. I like big trucks and the bad boys that drive them. Fast and hard. I want all of him, in every way. I want his cock fucking my pussy. Fucking my ass. And damn it that I don't have lube here and now, but two out of three is good enough.

I reach back, struggling to keep my balance with one hand and to move my arm since my shirt is wrapped tight around my elbow. But I find him. I tug the head of his cock forward. And, after a moment's hesitation, a moment where I know prudent, anal-retentive Nate worries about whether this is a good idea or not, he follows my lead. And I know why we're here now, a thousand miles away from the safe confines of our world. He trusts me.

Ready as I am for him, he has to coax me, open me up bit by bit. And, oh hell, no, he wasn't compensating for a goddamned thing. But then he's inside of me, every last inch, and his fingers are tight on my hips as he fucks me. He sighs my name. He snarls it. Harder. And I'm coming again even though my mind is telling me this is insane and I should be far, far past the point of satiation. It tells me I'm going to be sore as hell tomorrow, but I don't fucking care. And then with a final thrust he stills, and I feel his heart pounding like a trip hammer against my shoulder blade.

Once again I can hear the sounds of the wind and the desert, the drone of a prop plane far overhead, the faint whirr of the ice freezer out in front of the store. The sound of his breathing as his head rests on mine. When it steadies at last, he raises himself on his arms, still bracing against the car for support, and I lever myself upright.

Some ingrained sense of prudishness makes me shrug my clothes up over my shoulders and hook my bra. To hell with buttoning the shirt, and my stockings are history. I think I'll just swap the shirt out for a long-sleeved T-shirt from my luggage. It won't take but a look to know the reason for the state of my clothing – or, on second thought, maybe not. I suddenly like the idea of walking into the hotel lobby with Nate Marble and every single stranger who looks at us knowing exactly what we've been doing.

The thought brings a grin to my face and he looks up from belting his pants and grins back. Damp strands of hair fall over his forehead. The starch of his shirt has long given up the ghost and his cheeks are still flushed. That's beauty right there.

'Remind me not to get lost with you any more,' he says.

'Oh?'

'Yeah. I might be too distracted to ever get back.'

I laugh and roll my eyes. 'Don't worry, cowboy, I'll club you over the head and drag you back.'

'Quite the charmer, aren't you?'

He gives me a long, long look.

Finally, he turns and takes the patient nozzle out of the tank, replaces it on the lever. The pump beeps uncertainly for a second or two before spitting out a receipt. I button my shirt halfway, collect the bottles from atop the car and dump them in the bagless trash can beside the pump. Then I strip off my stockings one by one and send them after the bottles.

'All ready?' he asks.

I nod. 'Yup. But Nate . . . ?'

He turns in the act of walking around to open my car door and raises his eyebrows. A shadow of uneasiness crosses his face, like a little boy afraid of impending disappointment and trying his best to hide it.

I smile.

'Promise to take me for a ride in your truck.'

The shadow disappears. He smiles and my weary libido can't help but tingle in response. My heart can't help but flutter in anticipation.

'As many rides as you want, gorgeous,' he says.

'Good.' I brush my lips lightly against his as I get into the car and I hear his breath catch.

'And I promise not to let you get lost too often,' I add as he slides into his seat and closes the door. He laughs as he starts the engine.

Union Blues Monica Belle

Outside my window it was a perfect spring day, warm and sunny, with just the faintest breeze rustling the leaves of the plane trees along the Marylebone Road. Even the traffic seemed less urgent than usual, and above it the blue of the sky was marked only by twin vapour trails. One of the jets was still visible, a tiny arrow far above me. It was headed south and west, somewhere hot, maybe Florida, or Rio.

The buzz of the intercom on my desk brought me sharply down to earth, and the offices of West Central Railways. Mr Hawkridge's voice sounded from the tiny plastic grille, as if he had somehow been miniaturised and trapped within the office intranet, something I had fantasised over more than once.

'Frances? Come up to the boardroom, please.'

'Yes, Mr Hawkridge.'

I hadn't expected the call for a good five minutes, with the union meeting scheduled for eleven a.m., and he was normally punctual to the point of obsession. As the youngest man on our management team he seemed to feel he had a lot to prove. He also seemed to feel the need to exert his authority, calling me Frances while he insisted on

Mr Hawkridge. It was annoying, and all the more so because the way he behaved towards me put an all too familiar tingling sensation between my legs.

The boardroom seemed an odd choice for the meeting, with just a single representative from each of the three main unions in attendance. I'd expected it to be in Mr Hawkridge's office, but possibly he was hoping to overawe them with the formal, affluent atmosphere, or make them feel important, or whatever, but there would be a reason. Mr Hawkridge liked mind games.

One floor up, across the open floor of the main office, the low, constant hum of PCs and the air conditioning cut through with the gentle babble of voices gave way to the hush of the boardroom as I entered. Mr Hawkridge was already seated, in the high-backed leather chair normally reserved for the chairman. He waited until I'd closed the door before speaking, and I noticed that the slats on the internal windows were closed, cutting off the view of the main office.

'Frances, good. I wanted to speak to you before the meeting.'

His tone was clipped, precise, exactly as he was, with his tailored suit of fine, light-grey wool, his dove-grey silk shirt and perfectly knotted tie. There was just a touch of grey in his hair, but his strong, clean-shaven face was full of youthful confidence, also a hint of amusement, as if everything was no more than a game. He gestured to a seat, a plain black swivel chair placed unobtrusively in one corner.

'Do sit down. Now, as you know, I have a meeting scheduled with representatives from the three principal railway unions. At this stage, the negotiations are strictly off the record and, frankly, I think they're testing the water, this being only the second year of our franchise.'

He went on for a while, explaining that he wanted me to observe the meeting but deliberately not record what was said, my true function being to support him if the reps claimed that anything had been agreed when it hadn't, or presumably if he wanted to backtrack on something he really had said. I took it all in, nodding at the appropriate junctures while wondering if the meeting would drag on into lunch and spoil my chances of getting down to Hell on Heels during my break. There was a pair of zebra-patterned boots I just had to have and, with any luck, they'd be reduced to something approaching a sensible price.

Five minutes must have passed, because the intercom went to say the reps were coming up from reception. Two minutes later they filed in, by which time I had my laptop open on the desk, looking efficient and feeling slightly too hot. Company policy demanded smart dress, and I might have been Mr Hawkridge's little sister, style-wise, in my blue-grey two-piece, white blouse, stay-ups and sensible heels. With my hair up and my glasses on, I was everything they expected, my sole rebellion a pair of scarlet knickers in a heavy, luxurious silk – not something I intended to show.

I'd met all three reps before, men united only in their politics, and in being as out of place in the walnut veneer-tinged light of the boardroom as Hell's Angels at a scooter exhibition.

In they filed. There was big and brash Larry Ryan, B.U.R.W., part Irish, part Caribbean and part bastard – big, crude and forthright. I knew he fancied me; he took every opportunity he got to ogle my legs and chest whenever he popped into the offices. I wouldn't have minded, looks-wise, but he was always cutting me short, being condescending or patronising, presumably in an effort to get over his own feelings.

There was Jim Levens, U.W.R., young and keen and determinedly working class. I was sure his thick Manchester accent was put on, or at least exaggerated, and his principles more acquired than instinctive. He was lean, tall, with piercing eyes and an earnest manner, also the most intellectually aggressive of them, something which, like Mr Hawkridge's attitude, touched that politically incorrect spark of desire within me to submit and call him 'sir'.

Then there was Reg Davies, T.S.W.U., who acted as if he'd been around since the railways were nationalised, and looked it too. He was huge, over six foot, but square in bulk and with an enormous belly hanging out over the waistband of blue polyester trousers that had been developed over years of pie-and-a-pint meetings. I actually liked him for his down-to-earth cheeriness, although physically he was by far the least attractive. But at least he was friendly.

Each of them had brought his own particular, very masculine, scent into the room, and there was soon a heady collision of aromas: of smoky clothes and aftershave and testosterone. I was one girlie in the midst of a bunch of hulking, macho blokes, even if they did behave themselves these days. Since the introduction of politically correct working practices and a non-sexist working environment, I could tell that each one of them was bursting to be able to swagger and bellow, and fart and openly share their porn mags if someone gave them the liberty to do so. This tension made for a peculiar, and almost sexually charged, atmosphere.

'Good morning, gentlemen,' Mr Hawkridge greeted them. 'Do sit down. As you know, this is a purely informal, preliminary meeting, also confidential.'

'What about your secretary, then?' Larry Ryan asked, jerking a contemptuous thumb in my direction.

'Ms Tisbury Jones is my PA. Her discretion is absolute. As I was saying, this is an informal preliminary meeting, at which I hope to –'

'Make us back down,' Jim Levens interrupted. 'We won't.'

Mr Hawkridge raised an eyebrow.

'Should we not at least assess each other's positions?'

'The position is simple,' Levens answered him. 'The U.W.R. wants pay parity between drivers on driver-only trains and guards on dual-staff trains.'

'The position of the B.U.R.W. is also simple,' Ryan put in. 'We demand that the pay differential between guards on dual-staff trains and drivers on driver-only trains be maintained.'

'Then the issue would seem to be between your two unions?' Mr Hawkridge suggested.

'No,' both men answered as one, before Levens then carried on.

'We fully support our brothers in the B.U.R.W.'

Both Ryan and Reg Davies nodded their agreement.

'Mr Levens, Mr Ryan,' Mr Hawkridge said, sighing, 'that sort of bargaining strategy went out with the Callaghan government. You know as well as I do that what you're asking for is an impossibility. So, let's cut to the chase here. What is it you actually want?'

I began to let my mind wander, looking at Jim Levens's lean, strong hands, powerful yet sensitive, the hands of a working man turned to less physical employment. It was a shame we had to meet in the way we did, because it was not at all difficult to imagine those same strong hands on my body, being very tender, very careful, as if he was handling cut glass, his brilliant eyes full of worship and desire as he undressed me, garment by single garment.

Larry Ryan would be different. I knew what he wanted to do: to take out all his anger and inferiority on me, maybe throw me down on the desk, tear my blouse open, pull off my bra, wrench my skirt up around my hips, rip my knickers off and...

Only Reg Davies would pull him off, take me in his arms, comforting me, stroking my hair, at least until he lost control and pulled out his cock to make me take him in my mouth.

They were talking, an ultimately pointless discussion as they manoeuvred for advantage. Before long it had begun to get detailed, the provision of staff restrooms at stations, the company's new disciplinary procedure, nit-picking, dull. Surely there was something more worthwhile they could argue over?

'I hardly think Ms Tisbury Jones's, er, favours, shall we say, are relevant to the discussion.'

I looked up.

'I beg your pardon?'

None of them took the least bit of notice.

'The position of the B.U.R.W. is simple,' Larry Ryan was saying. 'We want perks, same as you get perks. I want a blow job from Fanny in the corner.'

My mouth came open in outrage, an outrage I could find no words to express.

'Gentlemen, really!' Mr Hawkridge responded, only to be interrupted by Reg Davies.

'Seems fair to me. I bet she goes down for you, eh, Bob?'

'I do not!' I managed, but Mr Hawkridge had gone red.

'Nah,' Jim Levens drawled, 'not a blow job. Public school, ain't he? He'd 'ave 'er dressed up as a schoolgirl. Knickers down over the knee for a good spanking, eh, Bob?'

'Mr Levens,' Mr Hawkridge said, with what I thought was amazing patience, 'if we could return to the matter in hand?'

'The matter in hand,' Larry Ryan answered, imitating Mr Hawkridge's accent, 'is that if we're to drop our demands for restrooms at Maidenhead, Slough and Henley, then I want your bird's gob around my cock.'

'Impossible,' Mr Hawkridge snapped. 'An outrage!'

'How about Reading?'

Mr Hawkridge paused for an instant before replying.

'Reading?'

'Yes, Reading.'

'But that's our secondary station, the savings –'

'Considerable, no doubt, but we of the B.U.R.W. are prepared to make that sacrifice.'

Mr Hawkridge glanced at me. I shook my head urgently, but it was obvious what was going through his mind. If the unions gave way on the installation of the Reading restroom we'd save thousands of man hours and tens of thousands of pounds. The reps had sat back, their faces absolutely earnest as they waited for Mr Hawkridge's response. None of them bothered to look at me, save for a glance at my chest from Jim Levens. Finally, Mr Hawkridge spoke.

'Ms Tisbury Jones ... Frances, I really feel that, in view of the concession Mr Ryan is offering, it would be in the best interests of the company if you were to suck his cock.'

'No!'

'Why not?'

'Why not? Because it's outrageous!'

'Ms Tisbury Jones, I wouldn't like to feel that you are being disloyal.'

'No, but ...'

'Consider the economic benefits to the company.'

'Yes, but ...'

'You wouldn't wish to prejudice the position of our franchise, I'm sure?'

'No, but ...'

'And no doubt there would be a little something in your Christmas bonus.'

'Yes, but ...'

'But what, Ms Tisbury Jones? We are all mature adults here, and I don't suppose it will be your first time.'

'No, but ...'

'There we are then,' he said happily. 'After all, what's one more little cock in your mouth compared to the good of the company.'

Jim Levens coughed and raised a finger. 'I must object to your use of the term "little", Mr Hawkridge, implying, as it does, a denigration of the working classes.'

'Don't sweat it, Jim,' Larry Ryan cut in, and casually pushed down the front of his trousers to pull out a truly monstrous package.

I swallowed, staring at the huge, dark shaft lying on his thigh, a good eight inches long, and as thick as my arm. He grinned. I could only stare at it, wondering how it would feel in my mouth, wondering if I could actually get my jaws open wide enough to do it. Mr Hawkridge gave a gentle cough, then spoke.

'Come along, Ms Tisbury Jones. As you know, I have another meeting scheduled for two o'clock.'

I nodded mechanically, and rose, unable to stop myself.

'Under the table, I think, Ms Tisbury Jones,' Mr Hawkridge stated. 'After all, we wouldn't wish to lay ourselves open to charges of impropriety, would we?'

'Under the table, yes. Impropriety, no,' I managed weakly.

I moved a chair. I got down on all fours and crawled in under the table. I found myself faced with Larry Ryan's open thighs, his monstrous cock in his hand, ready for my mouth. His chair was a little back, and I knew the others would be able to see, whatever Mr Hawkridge had said. I shuffled forwards, swallowing hard as I caught the thick, male scent of his cock. He looked down, grinning.

'Out with your knockers then, love, and get sucking.'

'No!' I protested, looking around at Mr Hawk-ridge in appeal.

'Having Ms Tisbury Jones expose herself is not part of the deal,' Mr Hawkridge pointed out.

'Bare knockers are a standard part of blow-job procedure,' Jim Levens insisted, wagging his finger at Mr Hawkridge. 'Ask anyone.'

'True,' Reg Davies agreed, nodding his head earnestly. 'It was always done tits out in my day.'

Mr Hawkridge glanced between the faces of the three reps, all of whom bore expressions of obstinate determination. He drew a sigh.

'If you could expose your breasts, please, Ms Tisbury Jones.'

I opened my mouth to speak, but shut it again. Five quick, angry motions and my blouse was open. Another and my bra catch was undone. One last and my breasts were bare. I took them in my hands, holding them up to show the men in the hope that I could instil into them at least a little of the shame they should have felt.

'There, is that what you wanted?' I demanded.

Larry Ryan nodded. 'Nice, nice ... not too big, not too small, very firm.'

'I like 'em small myself,' Reg Davies remarked. 'Nice and pert.'

'Nah, nah,' Jim Levens disagreed. 'Big is best, a working woman's breasts, full and heavy, good for child rearing.'

'That's bollocks,' Reg interrupted. 'Four kids my Linda's brought up, and her with a pair of fried eggs.'

'Do you mind!' I cut in. 'I am supposed to be performing fellatio.'

They went quiet. Jim Levens gave me a surprised look. Reg Davies shrugged. Larry Ryan lifted his cock up a little higher, offering it to my mouth. It truly was impressive, so thick his hand hardly closed around it. The head was big and solid and glossy; so suckable and, after all, it had to be done.

I took him in, my jaws gaping as wide as they'd go as my mouth filled with solid, meaty cock, right to the back, and not even half of it in. The others were watching and, as I began to suck, Reg Davies tucked his thumbs into his trousers, nodding thoughtfully as he spoke.

'I feel I must point out at this juncture that the restrooms under discussion are for the use of the T.S.W.U. and U.W.R. in addition to the B.U.R.W.'

'Perhaps we should allow Ms Tisbury Jones to deal with the matter in hand before moving on to further discussion?' Mr Hawkridge suggested, then gave a light laugh. 'Or perhaps that should be "the matter in mouth".'

I'd have given him a dirty look, but I was too busy performing my magic on the wonder tool of Larry Ryan. I was beginning to feel in need of some attention downstairs myself, and I was wondering if I'd have the time to fit Mr Hawkridge in before lunch. On the desk would be good, the way I always imagined it, with me on my back and my legs rolled up to let him in, nice and deep.

'As it goes, I'm not sure I can wait,' Jim Levens said suddenly.

'You'll just bloody have to,' Larry Ryan answered him with a grunt. 'I ain't rushing this.' Then he turned to me and said, 'Having a good suck down there, love? I'd love to do it all over your face. Ooh, you're going to make me come any second.'

I nodded on my mouthful of cock, took him as deep as I could one more time and moved down to lick at his sac and gently fondle his balls, rolling them over my tongue to make him gasp and shiver. Jim Levens gave a low groan.

'I've got to fuck her or I'm going to come in my pants. Be a mate, Larry, and move your chair back. I need some room.'

'Yeah, all right, but you'd better be quick.'

I was separated from Larry Ryan's equipment for a couple of seconds as he pushed his chair back on its rollers.

'Hey, no,' I protested, but Jim Levens was already pulling down his fly, to extract a long, pale cock, already erect.

'Skirt up, ducks,' he ordered, 'and don't worry, it won't take a minute.'

Mr Hawkridge coughed.

'I think not, gentlemen, at least, not without further concessions.'

'Fuck that!' Jim swore. 'Equal rights, that's what I want, and that's what I'm having.'

'No argument there, Mr Levens,' Mr Hawkridge said coolly. 'Once Mr Ryan has taken his pleasure with Ms Tisbury Jones, you may take yours, in her mouth, as previously agreed.'

Jim Levens's mouth came open, shut again, opened again, like a goldfish. Then he spoke. 'OK, you corporate running dog, what do you want?'

'This year's pay linked to inflation?'

'No way!'

'Frances, would you be good enough to lift your skirt?'

'But Mr Hawkridge . . .'

'Your skirt, please, Frances. I wish to demonstrate to Mr Levens precisely what he is missing.'

'But Mr Hawkridge . . .'

'Frances,' he said patiently, 'I really do think matters would be a great deal easier if you simply did as you were told, don't you?'

'But Mr Hawkridge . . .'

'Frances?'

I threw him a last, desperate look, but my hands were already on my skirt. All four of them were staring at me as I tugged it up, to show off my expensive scarlet silk knickers, and my bottom, most of which was spilling from the sides. I was already kneeling, which showed plenty, but pulled my back in a little to make the best of myself. I know how much men like to see that in-bending curve twixt breasts and hips.

'Fucking gorgeous,' Reg Davies breathed. 'Now that is an arse!'

Larry Ryan was leaning sideways out of his chair to get a better view, erect cock in his hand. He blew his breath out.

'What a peach!'

'Red knickers,' Jim Levens drawled. 'I love red knickers.'

'Stockings too,' Larry Ryan added. 'Real class. Stick it out a bit more, love.'

I threw him a resentful look but did as I was told, pulling my back in as tight as it would go.

'Fucking gorgeous,' Reg Davies repeated. 'There used to be this bird worked in the union president's office, back in the sixties it was. She used to wear red knickers and a skirt so short you could see 'em when she bent down. The Red Flag, the lads used to call her, and –'

'Mr Davies, perhaps if we could proceed?' Mr Hawkridge broke in politely.

Jim Levens stood up, rubbing his hands.

'The pay–inflation linkage, Mr Levens?' Mr Hawkridge enquired.

Jim nodded, his eyes never leaving my out-thrust bottom.

'For a period of five years?' Mr Hawkridge added.

'Five years? Fuck that!'

'No, Mr Levens, fuck that,' Mr Hawkridge responded, pointing to where my knickers were pulled tight over my pussy.

Jim Levens swallowed. His cock looked as if it was about to explode.

'OK, OK, five years,' he panted.

'Hold on just a minute, you're forgetting something here,' Reg Davies put in. 'What about the T.S.W.U.?'

'What about them?' Jim Levens demanded impatiently.

'Well, I want mine, that's what,' Reg answered him. 'And I'm not having your sloppy seconds, Jim Levens. Come on, love, pop your knicks down; you need a man for this job, not a boy.'

'Just one moment,' Jim snapped. 'May I remind you who has seniority here? Three times your members, I've got, Brother Davies, so I reckon that gives me the right to go first.'

'Seniority?' Reg Davies demanded. 'The U.W.R. may be the bigger union, but that does not mean you have seniority, my lad, not by a very long way indeed. Founded in eighteen-sixty-four, we were, eighteen-sixty-four.'

'By you?' Jim Levens enquired.

'I'm not that bloody old, you young pup,' Reg answered him. 'But, if you're to make an issue of it, I'll remind you that I was holding picket lines when you were in nappies, and before, so how about a bit of respect for your elders, eh?'

'Maybe you were,' Jim Levens retorted, 'but where were you boys the year before last when four of our boys were accused of kipping on the job, eh? That's what I'd like to know.'

'Secondary action, secondary action,' Reg Davies interrupted. 'And the lazy buggers were asleep, and all –'

'Are you saying my members sleep on the job?'

'I'm saying what I know, plain and straight.'

'Oh, you are, are you, well, just you –'

'Oh for goodness sake!' I yelled. 'One of you can

sodomise me if you really have to, but please stop arguing!'

All three men went quiet.

Reg Davies nodded. 'Seems fair.'

'Seems fair, brother,' Jim Levens agreed. 'Er . . . who goes where then?'

'I'm in the fanny, you're up the bum,' Reg answered. 'Stands to reason, that.'

'Why?'

'I need to go underneath, I do,' Reg asserted. 'On account of my weight and my age, you see. I haven't the puff I had when I was a young man. You, though, you look like you've the right equipment for the back door, so Fanny here, she climbs on top of me, like, and you slip it in up the back way, see?'

'Oh, right,' Jim answered, glancing down at his old chap. 'Come on then, Fanny, get 'em down.'

I nodded, feeling slightly weak, and reached back to pull down my knickers. They were going to get in the way so I took them right off and crawled forwards, to take Larry's cock in my mouth again as Reg lay down. I was watching him from the corner of my eye as I resumed sucking. Reg pulled his cock out, already hard for me, thick and stubby, maybe even thicker than Larry's, but not nearly as long.

He gave me a happy nod as he saw I was looking. I came off Larry and mounted up, straddling his huge hips to ease myself down on his erection. He fitted me beautifully, and I couldn't help but sigh as my pussy filled, right up, bringing me that wonderful, glorious, incomparable sensation of being really open around a big man's cock. He was so comfy too, like being mounted on a well-stuffed sofa, only a sofa I could fuck and fuck and fuck.

I'd begun to bounce up and down, I couldn't help myself. His huge tummy was right on my pussy, which was very rude, but it was going to make me come, and soon. Larry wheeled his chair in closer, beside me, and I opened wide to take him in, sucking happily as I rode Reg's cock. I could see Mr Hawkridge, sat back with a satisfied smile, steepling his fingers over his stomach, his eyes firmly on the junction between my mouth and Larry Ryan's cock.

'Hold it still a minute, ducks,' Jim said, as his long, strong hands closed on my hips.

He gripped tight, holding my bottom for penetration. I felt his cock touch me between my cheeks. I felt myself open. I felt myself fill, and all three of them were in me – three rough, tough, working men, sharing me, their lovely hard cocks in my body, my mouth, my bum and pussy, all at the same time. It was so good, perfect, and, as they began to get their rhythm inside me, I knew I'd be coming in just seconds. They'd taken over: Larry's hands in my hair as he slid his huge cock in and out between my lips; Jim in my bottom so deep I could feel his hair tickling between my cheeks; Reg filling me completely, pussy stretched so wide and pressed hard to his flesh, so good ... so good I was already coming, and, if I hadn't had a good six inches of thick brown cock in my mouth, I'd have screamed the building down.

As it was, I gave a little muffled gasp as, through the angle of my skirt, I discreetly pulled the ridge of my panties tightly over my clit for about the hundredth time for the past fifteen minutes. I was actually coming, licking my lips as I did so, revelling in the delicious explosion in my knickers.

'I beg your pardon, Frances, did you say something?' Mr Hawkridge asked.

I looked him in the eyes, my cunt still pulsing between my legs. 'No, no, nothing at all, Mr Hawkridge,' I replied as I snapped out of my daydream and back to the mundane reality of the union meeting. 'I was just thinking how we might resolve this issue.'

Monica Belle is the author of the Black Lace novels *Noble Vices*, *Valentina's Rules*, *Wild in the Country*, *Wild by Nature*, *Office Perks*, *Pagan Heat*, *Bound in Blue* and *The Boss*

Cabin Pressure Maya Hess

Natalie Beauman watched from the jump seat as Dubai disappeared into the desert. The ochre landscape was soon replaced by a mountain range she had never heard of and then the view from the porthole transformed into the indigo expanse of the Gulf of Oman. Natalie unbuckled her harness while the 747–400 juddered its way through cloud and mild turbulence, causing her to momentarily lose her balance as she headed for the first-class galley. She briefly checked her appearance in the stainless-steel door of a locker, straightened her red and white neck scarf and clasped her hands together ready for duty.

'Shall I begin serving?' Natalie asked Angela, her superior. Angela turned and stared at Natalie with a taut facial expression. Her eyes flicked to Natalie's breast to read her name badge suggesting that she had already forgotten her name.

'Captain Wild always has black coffee with two sugars when we break from the circuit. You can serve him first and then return to help me with the bar.' Angela's face loosened briefly into a wry smile and she ran her finger over her own name badge, which was decorated with five small sparkling gems. Natalie mirrored the action, tracing her finger over her own undecorated badge. One day she hoped to make it to purser too.

'Sure,' she replied sweetly. 'I'll sort that out right away.'

Natalie busied herself preparing the captain's tray, adding a couple of Viennese biscuits and a linen napkin before striding confidently to the cockpit. All the weeks of intensive training were finally being put to good use and already Natalie loved her new job passionately. During the flight from London to Dubai, she hadn't had a chance to get to know Angela and the rest of the first-class team. She had been dealing out headsets and trays of food in economy and, unbeknown to her, had been requested to work in first class for the final leg of the journey to Sydney. Now, as she slid past Angela and another senior member of the cabin crew, she became acutely aware that the two more experienced women were vetting her every move, watching how she performed in detail. Natalie couldn't quite hear their comments as she knocked on the cockpit door but she certainly heard their amused laughs as she clicked the door shut behind her.

'Your coffee, Captain Wild.' She'd seen it many times before during training but now it was the real thing, now she was actually working for Voyage-Air and she was standing before the flight crew in the nerve centre of Boeing's most impressive aircraft. Natalie felt her knees give a little. Her eyes blurred as banks of lights and digital displays spewed technical information at her from all angles and her hands shook, causing coffee to pool in the saucer. If there had been a spare seat, she would have taken it. She had barely noticed that the captain, his co-pilot and the navigator were all smirking at her.

'Your reputation precedes you across the world, Jim.' The co-pilot winked at Natalie and took the tray from her. 'Nothing for us?' he asked, eyeing the single coffee disdainfully.

'Of course. I'll –'

'My name is not Wild. I'm Captain Wilkinson.' His voice was deep and assertive and filled with the confidence of having spoken across the skies to the entire world's air traffic control centres. The pilot loosened the harness that stretched across his broad black-and-gold-clad shoulders and removed a pair of impenetrable aviation sunglasses. Natalie lowered her eyes as the captain's gaze flicked casually over her.

'It's just that Angela said you were –' Again, more laughter from the flight crew.

'Angela Cartwright is allowed to call me whatever she wishes.' Captain Wilkinson took a sip of his coffee and nodded in approval. 'She's earned her stripes.'

Natalie suddenly felt like her clothes had been removed and her skin was being abraded by the Captain's now scouring eyes. She wanted to take orders for the other drinks but stupidly felt rooted to the spot and quite unable to speak. Captain Wilkinson surveyed every part of Natalie, from the neat chignon secured by Voyage-Air's red and white pillbox hat, right down her sheer-stockinged legs to her patent red court shoes.

'You're new, right?'

'Yes, sir,' Natalie replied.

'Has Angela informed you of the initiation process yet? It's something we do for all new recruits as a kind of . . .' The captain's voice trailed off and he turned to his controls, making several adjustments to various instruments. 'Straight and level at thirty-three. See to the cabin announcements would you, Alan?' Captain Wilkinson turned his attention once more to Natalie. 'Call it a kind of welcome. As one of Voyage-Air's longest-serving captains, I like to get to know all my long-haul crew personally.'

Natalie relaxed and smiled. 'Shall I bring more coffee?'

The co-pilot and navigator gave her their requests and then swiftly resumed their duties, speaking a language punctuated by figures, safety checks and radio static. Natalie returned to the galley, assisting an elderly and extremely fussy passenger along the way. She wore her smile as stoically and genuinely as she wore the prestigious uniform of Voyage-Air.

'You look gorgeous. Did he love you?' Angela's stiff tone had dissolved and she gave a classic stewardess smile, elevating her otherwise determined features into a moment of camaraderie.

'Who?' Natalie frowned.

'Captain Wild, of course. He's the one that requested you work first class to Sydney.' Angela regained control of her professionalism and strode away from Natalie with the drinks trolley. Further down the aisle, she turned and delivered a slow wink to her bemused associate while trailing her finger over her gem-decorated badge.

Five hours into the flight, when the first-class passengers were fed and most of them reclined and dozing from too much champagne, Natalie lowered the cabin lights. There was a satisfied atmosphere aboard the aircraft. Exhausted herself, Natalie wouldn't have minded curling up in one of the luxurious seats and settling into a movie. She was desperate to kick off her heels and let down her tightly pinned hair and the prospect of a hot bath was as far away as the hotel in Sydney itself. As proud of it as she was, Natalie was desperate to shed her Voyage-Air uniform. Her intensive training had covered every aspect of long-haul work but had done little to prepare her for the exhaustion she was now suffering. She wondered if she'd ever get used to leaping across the time zones.

'I'm going for my break now. I'll be half an hour and then you can take yours. Shelley's also on duty so ask her if there are any problems.' Angela strode to the rear of the cabin and descended the small staircase, her long legs scissoring down the narrow aisle. Natalie decided to take another walk around the first-class cabin to make sure all her passengers' needs were met.

The old lady she had helped previously was now asleep with her head bent sideways at an uncomfortable angle. Natalie reached up into the overhead locker and took down a feather pillow and a satin-edged blanket. She skilfully positioned the woman's head on the pillow and only when she draped the blanket over her frail body did the woman stir and offer her a thankful smile. Natalie was filled with a feeling she couldn't explain. It was the sense of serving, without being subservient, that she relished so much.

'Excuse me.'

Natalie turned to whoever was whispering. In the subtle light she could see that a dark-haired man was beckoning to her and holding up his empty glass.

'Be a doll and get me another, would you?'

Natalie breathed in the sweet whiff of Voyage-Air's best Scotch as she approached the man. She considered advising him to take a large drink of water as she had already plied him with countless drinks over the last few hours. But he was behaving himself and appeared harmless and Natalie assumed that he would soon drift off into a deep sleep and wake up with a banging headache in Sydney. So she obliged him and returned with more Scotch and a tray of nibbles.

'Thought you might like these too,' she said as she lowered his table. Natalie struggled with the catch and the man's fingers momentarily collided with hers as he tried to help. Finally, the table opened.

'See,' he said. 'I'm not drunk at all.'

Natalie grinned, her face only inches away from

his. 'Did I say you were?' Politeness was imperative. The man's eyes narrowed, still at close range, and Natalie caught a flash of her scarlet uniform in his jet pupils. At first sight, he looked the most unlikely first-class passenger she had ever encountered. His hair was tousled and shoulder length, although undeniably charming the way it was pushed back off his tanned face, and he wore jeans and sneakers and a loose white shirt. Natalie had been surprised during boarding that, amongst all the designer suits and smart dresses and expensive hand luggage, this particular passenger had arrived wearing a beat-up leather jacket and carrying a vintage holdall. But it was not her duty to judge.

'Can I get you anything else, sir?' His perusal of her was both exciting and excruciating because Natalie knew in a flash what he was thinking, even before his eyes plunged into the gap between her dainty neck scarf and the V-shape of her fitted blouse. It was a leading question but one that had been drummed into her during the intensive weeks of training. She had asked it a hundred times already during the flight.

'Let me think,' he replied, his words now distinctly stretched by alcohol. Natalie waited patiently, although feeling more uncomfortable from the way his eyes soaked up her body at close range. 'A bed would be nice.'

Thankful for a reason to break the palpable tension between them, Natalie reached up to the overhead locker and retrieved yet another lavender-scented pillow and blanket. 'Your seat reclines almost horizontally. Here, just pull on this and push back hard.' Natalie immediately wanted to clap her hand to her mouth and scuttle off to the safety of the galley. She felt like a silly schoolgirl.

'It's been a while since anyone so delightful has said anything like that to me,' the man quipped predictably but he did as instructed and was soon lying on his back while Natalie dutifully arranged the blanket. 'Should I get undressed?'

'I'm sure that won't be necessary, sir. Once you get to sleep you'll find that we'll be in Sydney in virtually no time at all. I'll wake you when it's time for breakfast.'

'I'm surely in heaven,' he confessed, taking another sip of the Scotch, 'being tended to by an angel.' Natalie detected the faintest trace of an Irish accent in his voice, creating an arousing concoction as semi-coherent words drizzled from his mouth. 'Shame you can't climb in beside...' The passenger's head finally succumbed to the weight of tiredness and drink and Natalie plucked the glass from his hand and placed it on the table.

'That would be quite against company rules, sir,' she whispered as she walked away. A little part of her believed that he had spoken out of turn but – and she tried to deny this – a much larger part of her knew that she would have adored to duck under the blanket with him.

Half an hour later, Natalie left the first-class deck for her break. She entered the crew's tiny cabin, thankful that no one else was there, and clicked the door closed, then dropped down exhausted on the foldaway bunk. She could smell the remains of Angela's break – coffee mingled with reheated pasta and chicken from the economy galley. But there was something else noticeable, a tang that hadn't yet been extracted by the air conditioning. It was as if the walls, the oval window looking down upon the blackened earth, the bedding and even the food that had been left out for her were all drenched in it. An unfamiliar part of Angela had seeped out of her and condensed for subsequent crew to find and enjoy.

Natalie kicked off her shoes and lay back on the bunk. A chill drove through her body so she pulled the plain grey blanket over her and at once the smell intensified as if a whole bottle of it had been shaken out on the bed. It was the musk of Arabia, the scent of sun-kissed skin, the deep saltiness of the ocean thousands of feet beneath all blended to a frenzy with one unmistakable aroma. Natalie pressed the blanket to her face to confirm, then rolled over and breathed in the soft pillow. She trailed her fingers across the cool, slightly damp porthole and drew in what she already knew. Angela had just had sex in the cabin, either on her own or with another crew member. She smiled to herself and began to unbutton her blouse. There was just enough time and she was so tired that half an hour of sleep would never be enough. Already semi-aroused, she needed a sure-fire way to kick-start her energy levels to get her through to Sydney.

Natalie hitched up her slim red skirt and drove a finger behind her stocking top, easing it down her thigh. She began to work on the other leg but stopped as something unfamiliar caught on her hand. Rolling aside, Natalie retrieved a piece of soft and delicate fabric from under the blanket and could only assume, when she saw them, that the tiny black panties were a gift from Angela. Or a careless mistake, perhaps, at the end of a rushed and passionate tryst.

Either way Natalie smiled, now feeling as boozy as the man she had recently tended to in first class, especially when she recalled the way he had peered down her cleavage. She slipped off her blouse and released her bra, her tawny nipples waking suddenly from the jet of cold air from above. Natalie knelt on the bunk and stared out of the oval window at the world below. There was nothing much to see in the complete blackness, no one to witness her naked breast pushing against the cold window or her wetted finger circling a nipple that had begged to be touched since the flight began. Natalie's mind wandered back to the cockpit and Captain Wilkinson's hard jawline and tanned neck slipping comfortably beneath his starched white collar. In her current dishevelled state, she wondered what he would think if he saw her smart Voyage-Air skirt hitched up around her waist and her blouse thrown crumpled onto the floor.

'He'd have to tell me off,' she whispered to herself, fogging the glass. 'I definitely deserve a

punishment for being so naughty while on duty.'
Natalie giggled at the madness of it all. Here she
was, about to bring herself to a frenzied orgasm
at thirty-five thousand feet above Indonesia and
she was fantasising about what Captain Wilkinson would do to her. She was also quite unable to
rid her mind of the unusually handsome passenger in first class and, staring out into the void
below, she allowed her imagination to dive
beneath the satin-edged blanket covering him to
see just what was under there.

Natalie reached for Angela's lacy panties and
brought them to her face. Animal instinct told her
that she needed to know more and, by breathing
them in, she would be allowing the cool, crisp and
elegant Angela to affect her body. She touched the
delicate fabric lightly on her nose and drew in the
undiluted musk that she had first noticed filling
the room. Angela was a powerful woman and had
a strong scent nestling between her legs. Natalie
took a closer look. The tiny crotch was lined with
a single silver streak that glistened in the overhead light. It was the source of the aroma; a
marker of Angela's recent antics and proof that
she too was filled with the same desires that
working in such a close environment aroused.
Natalie allowed her tongue to pass between her
lips and glide over the honey spread on the panties. She closed her eyes and imagined that
Angela's long, lean body was pressed on top of
her with the sweet source of this heavenly taste
smothering her mouth. So evocative was the sin-

gle lick, so druglike in its effect that Natalie wanted more and more of Angela's juices. She traced her tongue along the silver streak again and eased her finger inside her own lace knickers and wondered if Angela's pussy felt anything like hers.

Forgetting the world below, Natalie dropped back onto the bunk. Wearing nothing on top but her neck scarf and scarlet hat, which had now lost its neat hold on her hair, she took off her knickers and slipped both ankles into Angela's little black panties. She pulled them up to her knees and circled her wet lips to get a dose of her own juice to spread with Angela's. The cabin door opened.

'So sorry to crash in on you like this but the captain's coming and –'

The two women locked eyes and in the same beat knew exactly what the other was thinking. Angela continued flawlessly, with only a small swallow to conceal shock or delight, and slid into the bunk room clicking the door shut behind her. In the same space of time, Natalie had quickly risen from the bed and pulled up Angela's panties as if they were her own. She already had her blouse over her shoulders.

'– and he's bringing his cousin for a tour of the aircraft. Better get shipshape, eh?' Angela offered a slow wink before turning her back and allowing Natalie to finish dressing. She was perfectly calm and professional, as if she was dealing with a nuisance passenger.

'I just needed to . . .' Natalie stammered. Her

cheeks flushed to match the jacket that she was now fastening and her legs trembled as she pushed her feet back into her shoes. 'It's not like you think, really...' Words were useless, Natalie realised as she struggled with her hat and unruly hair in the mirror.

'Here, let me help.' Angela trailed her fingers up Natalie's neck and pinned several loose strands in place. She leaned forwards, her mouth a whisper away from Natalie's ear, the firmness of her breasts nudging the other woman's back. 'It's OK. I understand.'

Again, the door opened and Captain Wilkinson and his cousin stood shoulder to shoulder in the narrow aisle. 'And this is where the crew take their breaks.' The captain loomed in the doorway, his sharp eyes quickly assessing the situation. 'Angela, what are you doing in here? Return to the upper deck immediately.' Angela nodded and slid between the two men. Natalie was left imprisoned in the cabin.

'I was just taking my break, sir.' Natalie finally had her uniform back in order and stared at the captain, fighting hard to keep her eyes off the other man – the man she had recently served with Scotch. Captain Wilkinson's eyes trawled around the small space behind her, lingering particularly on the dishevelled bunk. The thought that she had left her own underwear visible sent shock waves through Natalie. She thought she might be sick and cursed herself for such lack of control.

'It's important that you stay refreshed on such

a long haul.' The captain's words were clipped and disjointed, as if something else was occupying his immediate thoughts. He turned to his cousin. 'Would you like to take a closer look?' The captain glanced back down the aisle and then pushed up the gold-edged cuff of his jacket and looked at his watch.

'You know I'm fascinated by aircraft, Jim.' The Irish accent drawled long and slow, the words pouring over Natalie like his gaze. 'I'd be delighted to take a closer look.' The man steadied himself against the bulkhead and pushed his fingers through his long tousled hair. Natalie was reminded of a rock singer and fought to keep her eyes fixed on the captain.

'In that case,' she said, quite unable to understand their interest in the crew quarters, 'I'll get back to work and leave you two to your tour.' She made to slide between the men, as Angela had done, but was met with the captain's upheld hands.

'You misunderstand,' he said, gently nudging Natalie back into the tiny space. 'It's *you* we want to take a closer look at.'

Before she could grasp what was happening, Natalie found herself pressed against the cabin wall and her senses overloaded with fear, adrenalin, the tang of expensive cologne, freshly laundered clothing and, of course, the pungent whisky. Desperate to regain control of the situation, Natalie squeezed away from her captive position and began to laugh.

'I get it,' she said, barely able to speak. 'This is that silly initiation thing you told me about in the cockpit, right?'

'She's a bright one, don't you think, Carl?' To Natalie's horror, the captain was unbuttoning his jacket. 'And how rude of me not to make introductions. Carl, this is my beautiful new stewardess, Natalie Beauman. Natalie, say hello to Carl. He's my cousin and on his way back home to Sydney.' Captain Wilkinson waited while the two acknowledged each other.

'I've already had the pleasure, Jim. She's been an angel and only recently tucked me into bed.' Carl watched Natalie as he spoke, desperate to measure her reaction. There was nothing except for a tiny ripple in her throat as she swallowed.

'Yes, Carl has been keeping me busy with the drinks trolley.' Natalie opted for a light-hearted grab at freedom. She followed her comment with a lunge at the door. 'Aren't I initiated yet?' she asked stupidly. Instinct told her that they hadn't even begun. Natalie's heart pounded against her ribs, fuelled by adrenalin that raced to every part of her already aroused body.

'Like I told you, I get to know all of my crew personally. I find it helps working relationships hum along.' The captain had already removed his jacket and made a point of hanging it carefully on the back of the door. He broke the knot of his tie with one hand and unfastened the top two buttons of his shirt. 'I wasn't going to initiate you until we arrived in Sydney but Angela has been telling me how delightful you are and I simply couldn't wait.'

Natalie was stunned. She could only assume that the captain was about to force himself upon her, right here in front of his cousin. Again, that swell of nausea gripped her body, which mutated into yet another wave of anticipation. Her nipples still prickled beneath her bra from having tasted Angela so intimately without her knowledge and when she remembered that she was wearing the other woman's panties, she let out a little gasp that the captain obviously interpreted as one of compliance. He approached Natalie and drew a line from the tip of her nose, down across her left breast, over the gentle curve of her stomach, coming to rest between her thighs.

'Would you please remove your jacket, Miss Beauman, and unfasten your blouse.'

'Captain's orders?' she whispered, her voice stilted by the sensations building within Angela's lace knickers. Captain Wilkinson nodded and stepped back so that both men could see clearly while, with trembling fingers, Natalie did as she was instructed.

It occurred to her that if she didn't comply, she might never be promoted or at worst she could lose her job. When she had finished, the captain approached her and ran both hands down the exposed skin of her breasts. He pushed his face between Natalie's full curves and bit gently on the pale flesh nestled within her bra. Impatient for more, he removed her blouse and unhooked her bra, allowing both to fall to the floor with none of the respect he had shown his own uniform. At close range, he eyed Natalie's young breasts and took one nipple and then the other in his mouth, teasing them relentlessly into whipped peaks.

'Whoa, this is one hell of a tour,' Carl said, having to steady himself on the bunk. Natalie caught his eye but her vision was blurred, as if all her senses had been diverted to focus on the pleasure in her nipples. She was now quite unable to protest, even if she had wanted to.

'What were you and Angela doing in here before we interrupted you?' The captain stood upright and towered above Natalie. Before she could answer, he plunged his mouth onto hers and cupped the slightly askew chignon at the back of her head in his palms. 'Were you up to no good?'

Natalie gasped for air. 'No, I was just on my break and –'

'Did you touch her?'

Natalie was going to object but could see that was futile. The captain believed what he wanted and Natalie's job, as a loyal crew member, was to oblige.

'Yes, sir.' She hung her head.

'I can smell that you did. I can smell sex in here. The whole cabin reeks of it, you dirty little girl. I'll see to it that Angela gets punished later. But first, I have to deal with you.'

Before she knew what was happening, Natalie

felt her brand-new Voyage-Air skirt being torn from her waist. The captain had turned into a hungry wolf as the lacerated cloth was tossed aside. He clawed at her back, then swung her around and deposited her on the small bunk. The jet of air conditioning blasted on her semi-naked body, littering her skin with tiny goosebumps, which the captain took delight in licking away. Beside her, Natalie heard the impatient growl of Carl and the occasional exclamation of disbelief at what he was witnessing.

James Wilkinson knelt above his prey and surveyed the flesh beneath him. He took a quick glance out of the window, perhaps gaining a visual check on altitude, before trailing a finger around the rim of the lace panties. He frowned and rubbed the gossamer-thin satin.

'I didn't know there were underwear regulations too,' he said. 'You girls all wear the same knickers?' He glanced at Carl, who had now slumped to the floor and was visually massaging Natalie from head to toe. 'She's beautiful, isn't she?' he said before tearing the lace panties from Natalie's hips. 'So beautiful that I'm going to have to eat you from the inside out. But you keep quiet. We don't want to be disturbed.'

Natalie nodded obediently and arched her back involuntarily as the captain firmly drove a finger against her moist sex and then planted it on her lips, as if to seal her silence. She allowed her tongue a taste of her own juice, just to see if there was anything of Angela remaining. Natalie smiled and moaned as her neatly shaved pussy was nibbled and lapped at by the tongue of authority. The captain hoisted her legs up onto his shoulders allowing Carl a brief view of her entire sex, from the tight pink circle of her arse up to the sweetlike nub bursting from between her lips. Over and over, James drove his tongue in and around her engorged flesh, one minute hanging her on the edge of an orgasm and the next dropping her into a cataclysm of near pain as he bit and scratched at her buttocks.

'You taste so different to Angela,' he said, pausing to tease her nipples again. 'If Angela's a spicy Thai dish then you're a bowl of strawberries and cream. Do you like Thai food, Carl?' he asked, laughing and looking at his nearly passed-out cousin. 'I bet *you'd* love to share a hot and sour dish with me when we reach the hotel, wouldn't you, Miss Beauman?'

'Oh yes, captain,' Natalie replied, breathless at what he was going to do next.

'And you'd offer us dessert?'

Natalie moaned and lowered her hands to the captain's groin to indicate her reply. The size of his cock, buried within his neatly pressed black trousers, confirmed just how hungry he was. She unzipped him and lowered his clothing to reveal his erection but before she could do anything else, James had it in front of her face.

'What do you smell?' he asked.

Natalie took her time and traced her tongue around the head of the captain's cock. It took only seconds to discover the scent of Angela buttered all over him, that exotic tang which she secreted between her legs. Natalie grinned and began to take him in her mouth. Inch by inch she buried the captain of the 747–400 down her soft throat and ate up every trace of the elegant Angela. When it was all gone, consolation was that she knew there was more waiting for her when they arrived in Sydney.

Captain Wilkinson pulled away and looked at his watch again, then suddenly rolled Natalie onto her stomach in the confined space.

'You ready as we are, Carl?' he said with a laugh before taking hold of his cock and guiding it between Natalie's uplifted thighs. 'Final approach to land,' he joked before easing himself into the narrow but glistening channel Natalie was offering. He moaned loudly as he drew in and out, familiarising himself with the new territory and wanting to scream out as the tightness of Natalie's sex bit back at him. 'Steady, steady,' he ordered as her grinding hips dipped back and forth over his cock. Captain Wilkinson guided himself by gripping her slim shoulders, as if he was in command of a delicate glider in a cross-wind landing. He looked down to see the entire length of his erection being rhythmically pulled back into Natalie's perfect body, as if there was an undiscovered force steering him ever deeper. He delved high into her, relishing every involuntary contraction from her sex, convinced that if he pumped harder he would burst into her womb. He heard her breathing quicken, noticed how her knuckles whitened as she gripped the edge of the bunk, saw the lean muscles straddling her back tense in time with the contractions gripping his girth. Captain Wilkinson was a happy man as his aircraft cruised at thirty-five thousand feet.

'Oh stop, please.' Natalie pulled herself off James and shifted around to face him. 'I don't want to come yet. I want it to go on forever.' She took his milky erection between her fingers and kissed off all the wetness before planting her mouth over his.

'I think we'd run out of fuel if that happened,' the captain said, pulling off her kiss. 'And I haven't officially welcomed you to Voyage-Air yet.'

Natalie playfully tilted her head and massaged her aching nipples. 'Oh, and what might that entail?' Before she even had a chance to think, she was flipped around again and James's hands were underneath her flat belly, holding her firmly on all fours. She was overwhelmed by a sensation that she had never encountered before: a forbidden but delicious tingling that she had often fantasised about but never had the opportunity to explore. The captain's wetted finger was gently priming the entrance between her buttocks, easing inside by an inch or two. Natalie moaned but instantly felt guilty. Surely such an act shouldn't feel like this? Unable to help herself, she pushed back against his finger but was disappointed when he withdrew it. She wanted more and moved her hungry body around in search of the new and illicit sensation.

'You like that, huh? Well, how about this, then?' Captain Wilkinson took Natalie's breath away by nudging the virgin hole with the head of his cock. Natalie felt his warmth pulsing in this completely unfamiliar place and let out a little cry of pain as the first fat inch stretched her open. 'I'll go easy, honey, but you've got to let me in. It's the rules.' The captain laughed but then began to concentrate on fitting himself in completely. He ran his hands down Natalie's silky stocking-covered legs to her red patent shoes. The only other garments she wore were her Voyage-Air neck scarf and hat, with the rest of her uniform discarded in an untidy heap on the floor. James laughed inwardly. He'd lost count of the number of new stewardesses he'd welcomed into the airline. He reached a moist finger around Natalie's body to tease her tender clitoris and pushed his cock deeper still, skilfully working himself close to orgasm in only half a dozen strokes.

'I think you're going to do it, honey,' he whispered in her ear as the last clip fell from Natalie's hat, allowing her long blonde hair to drop around her shoulders. He plunged his cock as far as it could possibly go and held quite still for a couple of beats to relish the feeling of being on the brink. Natalie worked her arse in slow-motion circles, encouraging her captain to send more shock waves up inside her. She never wanted it to end.

Captain Wilkinson set to work on her jewel-like clitoris with his finger. He couldn't hold himself back any longer and wanted Natalie's orgasm to pump every drop from him. As capably as he controlled an aircraft, James guided Natalie towards the perfect climax. His weight dropped forwards, lowering her flat onto the bunk and pinning her in place while he finished the pounding from behind.

Her cries of pain from the size of him became moans of pleasure as she bolted through the hot rods of orgasm in a place she'd never felt it before. It continued for twice as long as she was used to and touched every part of her body, as if the captain had pumped her blood with a sex drug.

James finally came to rest, sweating and exhausted, lying on Natalie's back. He planted tiny kisses along her spine and wrapped her shiny hair around his fingers. 'The beginning of a very long and productive working relationship, I hope,' he whispered in her ear. 'You've certainly earned your stripes.'

Natalie wriggled around to face him. 'Stripes?'

James stood up, leaving a salty-cologne waft where he was lying, and breathlessly plucked something from his jacket pocket. 'These are for you,' he offered. 'Let me.' James picked up Natalie's scarlet Voyage-Air jacket and located her name badge. Underneath the letters of her name, he neatly positioned five sparkling gems. 'When you see any crew wearing these on their badge, you know they're one of mine.'

'And I thought Angela's gems were for long service or hard work.' Natalie smiled and watched the captain get dressed. She pulled her jacket towards her and ran her finger proudly over the glittering stones. 'It's like a secret club,' she said, giggling, but then she remembered Carl, still watching from his position in the corner.

'I've got an aeroplane to fly,' James said, buttoning his jacket and adjusting his captain's hat. 'But if there's anything else you need, Miss Beauman, I'm sure Carl will be happy to oblige.' He opened the cabin door. 'Oh, and take the rest of the flight off. You've earned it.'

Natalie giggled with delight as the captain left the crew quarters. Carl was already kneeling beside the bunk, quite happy to clean up the mess between the beautiful woman's legs and, moments later, he was mimicking the captain's actions inside Natalie's soft, melting pussy. Suddenly the pair lurched and nearly tumbled off the bunk as the aircraft's wings dipped sharply from side to side.

'Looks like we're in for a bumpy ride,' Carl said.

'That's not turbulence,' Natalie exclaimed. 'That's Captain Wild!'

Maya Hess is the author of the Black Lace novels *The Angels' Share* and *Bright Fire*.

Wet Walls Kristina Lloyd

The bus station was lit up with colour, rain falling in yellow and orange drops, headlights fraying into the drizzle.

I was trying to act natural, standing in the shelter like someone waiting for a bus. My real aim was to talk to the bunch of emo kids next to me, preferably without scaring them. A gang of moody youths with slanted haircuts, they might have intimidated some, but not me. I had them down as pleasant middle-class sixth formers, all dressed up and nowhere to go. Unable to think of a subtle opener, I came straight out with it: 'You know anything about this Michael guy?'

They turned to me with a disconcerting group mentality. Then they glanced at each other, a herd of scarecrow goths, anxious eyes flicking beneath angled fringes. Around us, reflected lights slid across perspex shelters and shimmered in fragments on slick black tarmac.

A skinny kid in drainpipes replied, 'You mean Michael Angelo?'

His tone was eager, and I immediately realised they knew less than I did. Just because they hung out on the streets, didn't mean they knew the streets. Obviously, they didn't think I was the police either. Or if they did, they didn't mind because they'd nothing to hide.

'It's well weird,' said another.

'Publicity stunt,' added a third, lighting a self-conscious cigarette. 'Got to be. How else do you explain it?'

I shrugged, turning away to check an approaching bus. 'Dunno. What's he publicising then?'

'Himself,' continued the third. 'Himself and fuck-all else. Same as everyone.'

There was a bubble of admiring laughter. See? Smart middle-class sixth formers.

A number 25 pulled in, tyres slushing through the wet, and I got on, then got off a stop later. They didn't know anything. There was no point me staying.

On Queen Street, I hurried into the Stationmaster's Arms, a place of seedy theatricality and pickled eggs. Men drank there; a thin crowd of commuters, dealers and pimps, as desperate and shabby as the pub's lost grandeur. Clenched and alone, they stood by the bar or sat at tables, eyes flinching from the deep dim mirrors.

I sipped a glass of red, head in a book, waiting for the shower to pass. I had no plan except to wander the streets in search of Michael Angelo. Or perhaps, given the email I'd received, he'd be out there searching for me. 'I'll find you in the darkest place,' he wrote.

I didn't know where that was, although the Stationmaster's Arms seemed as good a place as any.

I'm a journalist but, strictly speaking, this investigative stuff was way beyond my remit. I'm an agony aunt, writing the problem pages for a local property mag called *On The Up!* Problem pages, TV listings, lifestyle and other articles. That week, for example, I'd been writing a piece entitled 'A Day in the Life of an Estate Agent'. I'd been struggling with it, to be honest, because estate agents don't actually have lives.

But my problem page, oh boy, does that have life. And if it's ever flagging (because even problem pages have problems) then Mike and Aaron in design will offer me material. I never use it but it cheers me up. 'Dear Janie, What's the best way to remove hair from private parts?' or 'Dear Janie, My penis is too big. Please help.'

I wondered what letters the men in the Stationmaster's Arms might write, scribbling for help in the dark lonely hours. An old guy in a beige raincoat had been watching me, drinking steadily and offering an occasional smashed smile. His lank hair was nicotine yellow. I wondered if he could even write.

I confess I'm not cut out to be an agony aunt. I lack empathy and practicality, two attributes I'd say are fairly fundamental. Take the drunk in the raincoat, for example. Shouldn't I be wondering what damaged him and whether he might benefit from the twelve-step programme and some basic adult education? But, no. Instead I think: Sleaze-bag, get your eyes off me.

I only got lumbered with the problem page after Moira, our regular columnist, quit. She fell apart when her husband discovered she'd been having it away with his younger brother. 'Haven't I got enough problems of my own?' she used to yell, sobbing in front of her Mac, and I'm sure she'd have chucked letters around the office if all the stuff didn't come by email.

I inherited her desk. It's littered with self-help aphorisms: 'A ship is safest in harbour but that's not why ships are built'. Or 'A strong relationship is made not of two halves, but two wholes'. I crossed out the 'w' on that last word. Sometimes I think I inherited Moira's slump towards disenchantment. 'Haven't I got enough problems of my own?' I want to shout.

My problems, however, aren't as specific as hers. It's more formless stuff that goes on inside me, you know, at my edges and underneath. 'Dear Janie', I might begin, but then I'm pretty much stumped.

There's something I can't reach, a fluttery unsettled part I wish I could tame. Sometimes I feel I have it. It's almost there. For a moment it comes to rest, usually when I'm far from the city, and I'll be struck by, say, the light in a high golden barn or over a white wintry field where mist drapes the stubble. When that happens, I'm fooled by a fleeting sense into thinking everything's all right, now and forever.

But it isn't, is it? It's never all right. The days keep on coming and I can't get out of them.

There's nothing I can pin down. There are no sentences such as: 'I've got the blues' or 'My dog died' or 'I wish to God he'd leave me.'

Like I say, I'm not really up to agony-aunting.

Recently though, some of the letters have started to get to me. I'm puzzled and unsettled by them, and I know the usual platitudes I dish out won't suffice.

> Dear Janie,
> I don't know who else to turn to. I met a man recently and can't stop thinking about him. I know this sounds stupid but it was a one-night stand and he didn't ask for my number. We hardly spoke but I felt as if he truly understood me . . .

> Dear Janie,
> I've been going out with my boyfriend for eight months but I cheated on him at the weekend and now I don't know what to do. You see, I've fallen in love with this other guy though I know I'll never see him again . . .

> Dear Janie,
> I've been walking the streets at night, looking for a man I once had sex with. I know it's dangerous but I can't stop myself. I need to see his face. I didn't see it the first time and now I'm desperate to know him. It's like an addiction, an obsession, driving me on . . .

Dear Janie,
A man approached me on Queen Street after
I got off the bus and before I knew it, he'd
seduced me up against a wall. I thought
about going to the authorities but didn't
because he means everything to me, even
though he's a total stranger ...

Idiots! Get a grip, get a hobby, get a life.

I haven't published these letters though I've
read them so often I practically know them off by
heart. One line haunts me. It's there in every
letter, an unvarying refrain: 'With him, I found
another side to myself.'

I sipped my wine, aware I was still being ogled
by nicotine-hair. Perhaps he thought I was a
whore and that gave him the right. But what kind
of whore, I wondered, wears knee-length skirts
and flat-heeled boots, and sits with a glass of
Merlot, reading Barbara Vine? Not one he could
afford, that's for sure. It was time I left.

The rain had stopped and I headed up Queen
Street. It was early autumn and mild, the kerbs
stuck with wet golden leaves. Few people were
about. A couple of times I checked over my
shoulder but as far as I could tell, I wasn't being
followed.

I'll find you in the darkest place.

Was that a threat? Or the first sweet sting of
seduction? Either way, as I strode past glass-
fronted shops, the thought made me hot and
loose. He wanted me and I was scared to imagine

the possibilities of his wanting and the state I might be in when he was through.

In a recent half-page article for *On The Up!* I'd written: 'Michael Angelo might think he's an artist, but to many he's just a yob with a spray can. From boarded-up shops to newly painted buildings, no wall is safe from his defacement. The city is his canvas and we, the tax-payers, are footing the bill.'

I didn't actually believe what I'd written. Much of it was paranoia and sensationalism but I'm a hack, unschooled in truth and moderation. Anyway, these days people want a lot more than truth for their buck, especially in a property listings mag.

And the truth is, Michael's graffiti is beautiful. It has an astonishing luminosity, a softness that belies its weird jarring colours, and the first piece I saw of his brought tears to my eyes. ('Undoubtedly, his daubs have merit,' I wrote.) I was walking into work, crossing a dead-end street called Jubilee Gate and, when I glanced right, instead of the usual hoardings concealing the NCP car park, I saw a vista of paradise which briefly stopped my heart.

In a silvery sky, an olive-green sun shone over meadows of purple grass. Unearthly woodland clustered the hills, red-leaved canopies above cobalt-blue trunks. Snaking through the foreground was a river of molten copper, its shimmering bronze tones rippling with pink, and nodding in the breeze were fleshy daffodils of coral, apricot, vanilla and rose.

And yet how could there be a breeze? How could the river ripple? It was a painting, a mural perhaps, although mural is too flat a noun to describe the world I saw. It gleamed as if it were still wet. Perhaps it was. I walked towards it, feeling its dazzle of light on my cheeks. In its presence, I grew radiant, mesmerised by fierce magical colour, convinced I was on the brink of entering an altered, Photoshopped world where normality was oh so slightly out of whack.

There was a smell around me, a half-remembered scent. What was it? The closer I got, the stronger the odour until I felt quite engulfed by it. I inhaled deeply, filling my lungs, and my entire body tingled in response. Ah God, yes! Scents of sweat, skin and warm genitals unfurled in my brain. Sex! This world smelt of sex! I breathed in female arousal, strong and musky, and was embarrassed to think it might be me.

Worried, I glanced back. At the top of the street a man was gawping at the wall just as I was. I could smell cock and hair, so potent there might have been an erection by my lips, a jewel of pre-come quivering on its tip. My body answered, my groin its sudden centre of gravity, thrumming with an deep internal weight.

Ahead of me, paradise glimmered while behind me two people – the man and now a woman – glided towards the wall, equally dumbstruck. The three of us stared, steeped in that maddening air of lust. Did they smell it too? It was inconceivable we might speak, and yet the enchantment was such I could imagine us dropping to the floor and making mad crazy love, all three of us right there on the dead-end street that is Jubilee Gate.

Obviously, I didn't write this in my piece on Michael Angelo.

I stayed staring for several minutes while slowly, imperceptibly, the image and scent began to fade. By the time I walked away, it was just another example of very good graffiti, Michael Angelo's tag in the bottom right-hand corner. Perhaps good graffiti was all it ever had been.

And yet it left me in a state of desire so acute I felt demented. I could barely move. My vulval lips were exquisitely tender, so plump and soft that simply walking roused me further. Pavement to pussy, pavement to pussy; the rhythm drummed in my veins. I was all groin and longing. Each step cranked me higher until, aching for release, I had to nip into the ladies' in Starbucks to have a little wank. Or perhaps, given the locale, I should call it a regular and upgrade my normal fare to a grande.

That didn't go in the article either.

I only wrote the piece in the hope he would respond. 'Perhaps someday,' I declared, 'Michael Angelo will show us all another side to himself.' It was a weak bit of rhetoric and I wasn't happy with the sentence flow either. But I let it pass. The point of it was to try to prove my hunch that the letters and graffiti were connected.

Several days after the article appeared (I guess he's not a regular reader), I received his email: 'I'll find you in the darkest place.'

I'd trembled at the sight of his name in my inbox.

Michael Angelo.

The man. The mystery. Artist, vandal and demon lover.

I'd brought him closer. He'd come to me. He who did things to women, changing them utterly. The two men were one and the same, I was sure.

Despite my journalistic impulse to try to tempt him into disclosure, I didn't reply.

A couple of weeks later, he got in touch again: 'Won't you come out to play tonight?'

By then, the rumours were really starting to spread. Michael Angelo was no ordinary street artist. His pictures were alive; they breathed; they touched people in unspoken ways. He sprayed his walls in about five minutes flat; his tiny stencils sprayed themselves; those paintings of shadows might not even be his. He was a ghost, an angel, a con artist. He didn't even exist. It was a stunt dreamt up by a record company.

Then there were the rumours about him and women. He preyed on them. They preyed on him. You could feel the pull. Women loved him. Women hated him. He stole their shadows. Six were having his baby. He was actually Jesus Christ come to save us from ourselves.

And he'd asked me to come out to play.

I'd been feeling kind of spacey ever since I'd

first seen that wall. It was as if there was a newness in the world, a place of sensual tranquillity waiting to be explored. Desire and hunger spun me around, and I swirled in the midst of it, losing myself in daydreams where I floated among fingers or drowned in a sea of kisses.

Why, of course I'll come out to play.

I started off at Jubilee Gate but there was nothing to see now except the hoardings of the NCP car park, drab and ugly in the feeble streetlight. I visited other sites, looking out for broad canvases and small botanical stencils. I love his stencils. He sprays pictures of weeds, replacing the real groundsel, ragwort and valerian, removed by the council using deadly colourless sprays, with his own unnatural depictions. His counterfeit weeds grow from cracks in the pavement, and why not? Weeds have as much right to be in cities as they do in the countryside where they're known more prettily as wild flowers.

Michael's bigger pictures, the weird gaudy landscapes, usually vanish within days but the weeds last longer. There are hundreds of them, vibrant splashes of fake flora springing up across the city, ignored by passing feet. I'm not even sure if they're all his any more. It's as if the images are self-seeding.

I'd become something of a Michael Angelo fan, hurrying across town when I heard a new one had been spotted. Though I'd marvelled at the artistry, even getting down on my knees to sniff some weeds, none had affected me as much as the first one. That was the real start of my journey.

I'd been walking for about an hour, eyeing all men suspiciously, when the rain came on. At first, I considered quitting but, after lurking in the bus station, I decided to keep going. My guess was, if he was going to reveal himself, I'd need to be in a place considerably darker than those I'd checked out so far.

Fortified by that glass of red, I walked away from the centre, brain trying to convince gut I should head for the city's edge. It was desolate and lawless on the outskirts, an urban wasteland of burnt-out cars, 60s tower blocks and cold grey concrete, all newly animated by layers of graffiti, a palimpsest of rage and disaffection. The thought of going there scared me, especially since I'd written an article slating Michael Angelo. Perhaps he, or his fans, would want to take revenge.

Thankfully, as I was passing Upper Marlow Street, an area famed for its international cuisine, I had a sudden change of heart. It might have been the sight of people dawdling in front of menus and cosy windows, the smell of garlic or coloured lights on wet pavements. Either way, a buzz of excitement made me linger and, before long, I found myself gazing down Lower Marlow Street, a dark narrow road running behind the restaurants.

It felt like a place he might lurk. It felt right. The back ends of kitchens cluttered one side, a jumble of sloping roofs, bricks, stucco, extractor fans, thick silver pipes and stern, blank fire doors. Wheelie bins and crates lined the wonky pavement and, seeing no one else around, I walked forwards, nervous and alert. A few feet in, the solid hum of ventilation enveloped me, muffling the world. Small windows obscured by grids, grilles or frosted glass glowed softly, and I caught only snatches of kitchen life: a UV fly-zapper, shelves of packaged noodles, a corner of stainless steel; small, still images at odds with the feverish industry of scouring, clanging and sudden sizzles of fat.

It was like being in the cab of a steam train, seeing the furnace that fuels the city. Upper Marlow Street was civilisation; a place where appetites were whetted and quenched amidst tasselled menus, chopsticks, peppermills and candlelight. Here, behind the scenes, was the dark grubby truth of it.

The road was little more than a gap between old rickety buildings, street lamps along its length offering a faint white haze, as muzzy as gas lanterns in Sherlock Holmes' day.

'I'll find you in the darkest place.'

It was here. I could feel it in my bones. And yet, having arrived, I wasn't sure I could go on. What did he mean by finding me? And did I even want to be found? My heart was hammering and I almost turned back. Not so tough, after all. I could go home, put the telly on, rustle up an Ovaltine. But I was always doing that, wasn't I?

So I continued, walking along the pavement opposite the kitchens and bins, glints of mica on the ground sparkling in the half-light. The steady tap-tap of my footsteps reassured, a noise to pierce the dead murmur of ventilation. I passed walled backyards, doors, gates and alleys, the former tradesmen's entrances to once elegant townhouses. There wasn't a soul around, and I wondered if I'd been mistaken. Maybe this wasn't the place after all.

And then I saw him. Or I saw a man, menacingly still. Several yards ahead, he stood within a doorway, a slim youthful figure, a pale hoodie concealing his face like the cowl of a ghostly monk.

My heart skipped a beat. He didn't move a muscle though he must have heard me. I kept walking, anxiety tightening my throat. Head bowed, hands in his pockets, he stood beyond a pool of lamplight, faceless, hunched and furtive.

Afraid of him, I considered crossing the road but didn't, my main reason being a ridiculously British one: it might appear rude. I wondered how many die from politeness. I wondered too, what his pockets contained. Blood roared in my ears, matching the roar of ventilation as I dared myself to continue. Was I brave enough to walk past him? Stupid enough? And what if he wouldn't let me pass?

He was wearing trainers. His feet were quite large. The laces were tatty. His jeans were frayed. And then the feet moved, off the step, and he was out of the doorway, swaggering ahead, his stride quick and shifty.

I followed without a thought. His footsteps barely sounded while, behind him, mine clipped to keep pace. My mood soared, pulse drumming as I watched him walk, a touch of arrogance in his stride, droopy jeans and a neat little arse. Oh, he could lead me a merry dance around the city and I'd happily focus on that.

Seconds later, he threw a glance over his shoulder then darted into a narrow opening. Gone. In a heartbeat, I was with him, my breath coming in quick shallow gulps. He was there waiting for me. We stood in a shadowed entrance leading to a courtyard cluttered with fire escapes, stucco crumbling from its walls. He kept his head dipped, face concealed by his hooded top, and I simply stared, breathing hard.

Neither of us moved.

Then, 'Michael Angelo,' I pronounced.

Without raising his head, he swayed a fraction before taking a step towards me, shy and gauche. Instinctively, I backed away though something swelled in my heart and cunt. He stepped forwards again to stand perhaps a foot or more in front of me, that gentle pitch and roll in his stance reminding me of a landlubber on deck. I saw hints of a face, pale and angular. His manner was unthreatening, and there was a humbleness in the way he stood, as if he were presenting himself for my approval.

'Who are you?' I whispered.

He wavered a couple of inches closer, and I read it as an offering. Nervously, I reached out, slipped my hands under his top and edged him nearer, my tentative caress sliding over smooth taut skin. Oh, did he feel good beneath my fingers. He didn't respond. He simply stood there, taking it. My hands moved faster, firmer, my confidence rising with his apparent acquiescence. His body felt so healthy and alive, warm resilient skin skimming beneath my touch, muscles shifting as he swayed. His low-slung jeans rested on slender hips and I nudged his loosely belted waistband, palms pressing on the sweet jut of hip bone as my fingers kneaded his flesh.

'You're lovely,' said a soft, stunned voice, and I realised it was me.

I wanted to kiss him. My lips felt lost. But how could I kiss a man who wouldn't show his face? I could have peered into his hood but I resisted, not wanting to scare him. I settled, instead, for letting my hands explore.

It appeared to suit him. He seemed a passive, pleasured creature, allowing me to do what I wished. When I pushed his top high, he didn't object, and I gazed at the beautiful exposure of his body, at his flat honey-tanned stomach, athletic chest and the hair rising from his crotch like a thin line of smoke. His top slid up and down as my hands roamed, my lust snagged between the urge to touch and the hunger to see.

He didn't even squeak, not a grunt, groan or a hint of a gasp. How far might I go before he offered a response, some hint of sentience hidden within the hood? Where was this leading? I was open to all eventualities: he could leave, become aggressive, reveal a face I disliked or even one I knew. For him to be familiar was the most dreaded option. With this strangely docile, rag doll of a man, I felt far and away from anyone I'd ever known.

'Is this OK?' I breathed and, when he didn't reply, I let a cautious hand drift to the great lump of his groin. Still no complaint, especially not from me. Lightly, I stroked the shape of him, so turned on to feel the angle of his cock, its stiff urgency nosing at his jeans. I grew bolder, moulding the soft denim to his shaft, feeling how thick and hard he was. Yes, this was definitely OK. He didn't need words to tell me.

When I delved into his jeans, I discovered he'd gone commando, and the thick meat of his cock jerked to my touch. I curled my fingers around him and, at last, a tiny groan escaped his lips. I melted, bones dissolving in a sudden flood of lust. Within my fist he was vibrant and strong, and I reached deeper for his balls, straining for more sounds as I cupped his sac, toying with his shifting weights. Soon, I heard another faint murmur.

Just that noise, that hint of arousal and vulnerability, had me melting in another surge of wanting.

'Ah, fuck,' I gasped, feeling weak in the knees.

He edged closer, head rocking like someone half in a trance until, when I raked greedy fingernails down his back, his head lolled on a softly hissed breath. His hood slipped a little and, for the first time, I saw his face. Oh, and what a face it was. He had the most beautiful features, the flawless skin and sculpted clarity of someone noble or angelic. Light and shadow shifted within his hood, the gleam of the street casting a sheen on his narrow nose and the upsweep of his cheek. Stubble glittered darkly on his jaw and his eyes were deep set, a small ring glinting in one eyebrow.

Quickly, he looked away, shuffling closer, pushing his body against mine and making me stagger. I freed my hand, needing to balance.

'Careful! Stop it!' I said, but he kept going until I was pinned to the wall, his body pressing into mine, face averted. He clasped my wrists in each hand, then raised them high against the wall. Fear chased my lust, making my heart gallop, my breath quicken, but I didn't struggle, though I was braced in case I needed to.

I couldn't imagine needing to. We seemed to be fading into a world that was weirdly distant and yet somehow the same. While I was lucid enough to understand I ought to be on my guard, I was content to let it all happen. It was as if our here and now existed just centimetres to the left of ordinary. If anyone passed our courtyard alleyway, I imagined they wouldn't even see us. Here, it was all OK. I would wake up before anything bad happened, no problem.

Then, without turning to me, he spoke. His voice was a soft seductive breath. 'Is this what you want?'

I didn't reply. I could barely speak. The question

hung in the air and I stood, chest rising and falling, sandwiched between him and the wall, my arms splayed high in his grasp. Oh yes, I wanted this. I wanted whatever he had to give. I was wide open and reckless, liquefying in his presence. I wanted this, I wanted him, I wanted everything in the world. And soon, very soon, I'd find the words to say that.

'Ah,' I managed.

Still holding me, he leant towards my left hand and, with slow precision, he licked along the inside of my wrist. His tongue moved over delicate veined skin, flat and wet, and a shock of lust darted from my wrist to my groin where it flared to a wild eager pulse. I gazed into the courtyard, scanning small quiet windows. Hints of streetlight shone on black fire escapes and a chained-up bike, and from a washing line dangled an empty bird feeder. I couldn't see anyone peeping but I hardly cared. Michael Angelo had me pinned to the wall and he was licking my other wrist, slow and wet, the wedge of his cock shoving above my hip.

'Yes, I want this,' I whispered, his saliva cooling on my wrists.

'Then turn around,' he replied, releasing his grip.

He stayed close and I had to squirm to face the wall. Immediately he grabbed my hands and held them high again as if he were about to frisk me. I stood with my cheek to the stucco, his body a light pressure behind mine. The wall was rough to touch, the scars of old ivy draped there like giant grey lace.

In my ear, he murmured, 'I paint pictures.' His breath warmed me, then he tongued behind my ear and nibbled my lobe. I could hear the click and snuffle of his closeness, feel fabric brush my neck, and he pressed harder, his cock digging into my buttocks, forcing my pubic bone against the wall.

After a while, I said, 'Yes. I like them.'

He released my hands but I kept them there. 'I know you do,' he whispered, and he scrunched my skirt, bunching it higher until I felt the night air on the back of my bared thighs. He slipped a hand between my legs and rubbed the flesh there. I groaned, a noise like pain, as wetness sluiced through me. His fingers caressed my thighs, and I felt as if my cunt might dissolve down into my legs in search of his touch.

'Please,' I breathed, 'do something. Touch me. Fuck me.'

I leant heavily against the wall, needing its support, arms still raised. He edged my knickers down, firm hands skating over the globes of my arse, and I was so tense with wanting I almost stopped breathing. His fingertips stirred wisps of my pubes and inside I was aching, desperate to take the full fat thrust of him. I stepped out of my underwear, pushing my naked arse back.

'Hard,' I said. 'Do it hard. Please.'

He reached around to the front of me and rolled my erect clit, while his other hand squeezed and nipped my buttocks.

'Please,' I said in a near growl, and he clasped my waist, then jerked my hips back so I was tipped forwards, hands to the wall, hearing the sound of him unbuckle.

'I'm a stranger,' he said, and then the big head of his cock was there at my entrance, easing into my wetness. 'You came looking for me.' With a jolt, his cock slithered straight up me, my flesh rushing open. I was suddenly stuffed with meat, my hole stretched around his thick forceful girth, juices spilling. He shunted into me with slow deep thrusts.

'You walked alone down empty streets,' he said, speaking in quiet huffy breaths. 'And now a man you don't know fucks you against a wall. In the darkness.'

I panted and moaned as he rammed himself faster, keeping me close with that arm around my waist.

'You found this place,' he said, gasping a little. 'Not me. You found it. You're here, getting fucked, liking it, letting it all go. Blank, seedy, anonymous.'

I whimpered, his words making me flush. He was telling me how dangerous and dirty this was. I knew damn well I was at the mercy of how he might use his muscle and, while the prospect frightened me, I couldn't, wouldn't break away. He groped my breasts as we fucked, rummaged under my top, shoved aside my bra, pinched my stiff nipples. I loved the feel of him inside me; loved the furious thrust of him; loved the greed of his hand; and loved, most of all, being scared out of myself and flung into a place of debasement and abandon.

'There's a dark beauty in this, isn't there?' he said. Still thrusting, but slowing the pace, he leant forwards to bite my neck, teeth gently scraping. 'Filthy bitch,' he whispered, and he made the words sound so kind. 'Hot little cunt. Out looking for it. Chasing cock down the street.'

I groaned, an awful plaintive sound, and he dropped his hand to strum my clit. My orgasm began to tighten. My head span with hallucinatory colours, bright, beautiful landscapes and crazy phallic daffodils. I knew I was losing it, falling headlong into a tumble of warping ecstasy.

'You don't know who I am,' he said. 'And I'm fucking you, making you come.'

My body flared with sensation, my cunt dense with cock, heat, nerves and sodden, slippery friction.

'I'm making you come,' he panted as he butted at the core of me. 'Fucking you. Banging you. My hot little slut. She's coming. I'm making her come.'

His words rippled up my thighs and then I was coming hard, starbursts of colour exploding in my mind as I whimpered and wailed. He slowed, letting my climax grip, my inner walls clenching on him while the rest of me dissolved. Then, as my spasms faded, he shoved fast and rough before whipping himself clear and spurting on the ground. He came with a strained growl that thinned to a yelp. Suddenly I was afraid to turn. What the hell kind of noise was that?

My skirt dropped into position and I leant against the wall, panting. I could see the shape of him moving behind me, feel the brush of his movements, hear the shuffle of his feet. His breath was ragged like mine, and I felt its heat on my skin as he leant to print a kiss behind my ear.

'Goodbye.'

And then he was gone.

'No,' I pleaded.

I didn't see, hear or sense him go.

He simply wasn't there any more.

It was just me, breathless and stunned, violently alone. I stood, tender, sticky and dishevelled, in a grubby alley off a gloomy street.

Confused and a little hurt, I bent to hitch up my knickers. Typical bloody man, I thought, failing to convince myself. Then my heart lurched because the ground by my feet was glowing with bright pearly light. My boots were in a lime-lit mist, a blaze of white smoke illuminating concrete and stone. Afraid, I staggered away, turning to look. Weeds were growing up the wall, actually moving, hyper-real weeds in brash aerosol colours. Their leafy stems wriggled, their garish flowers pulsed, the patch emitting a strange phosphorescence as if a piece of moon had landed.

I clamped my hand to my mouth, edging back to view more of the wall. It was impossible, all of it. Rising from the weeds, dark against the pale scarred stucco, was a life-size silhouette of a woman, legs apart, hands spread in surrender. Me.

I thought of those terrible shadows left on

Japanese walls after the hottest flash. And even as I thought that, the image seemed to shift to become something more crystalline, atomised. Was it sprayed? It glimmered wetly but I didn't dare touch it. I could see my skirt bunched around my hips; the shape of my boots; how my hair had got messy; the way my mouth must look in profile when I cry out in ecstasy.

Even now, I struggle to find words for it, and words are my trade. A simple dark shape and yet it felt so intricate. It had a delicate, evanescent quality, despite its solidity.

No, that won't do, that won't do at all. Nothing will fix it. Nothing will describe it.

I felt as if I were in the presence of an extraordinary vision.

I felt as if my life had changed.

I felt scared yet elated and I backed away faster, panic rising.

Was this what they meant by another side? With him . . .

Would it fade? Would it vanish like the walls?

Dear Janie, I thought. Dear Janie . . .

And then I didn't know what to say. Because I didn't know if she would listen.

And even if I screamed, I didn't know if I'd be heard.

Kristina Lloyd is the author of the Black Lace novels *Darker than Love*, *Asking for Trouble* and *Split*.